Jester Average Murder

Copyright © 2025 Patti Petrone Miller All rights reserved

The characters and events portrayed in this book are fictitious. Any similarity to real persons, living or dead, is coincidental and not intended by the author.

No part of this book may be reproduced, or stored in a retrieval system, or transmitted in any form or by any means, electronic, mechanical, photocopying, recording, or otherwise, without express written permission of the publisher.

Cover design by: Pixel Squirrel
Printed in the United States of America

Patti Petrone Miller

Authors Book List

Accidental Vows
A Krampus Christmas
Sin Takes A Holiday
Barking Up The Wrong Bakery, Thankgiving
Barking Up The Wrong Bakery, Christmas
Best Served Dead
Bewitching Charms
Christmas at Hollybrook Inn
Christmas on Peppermit Lane
Krampus
Hex and the City
Love in Stitches
Pies and Perps
Spectres and Souffles
Mamma Mia It's Murder
Once Upon A Christmas
The Fatman
The Frosted Felony
The Purr-fect Suspect
The Boogeyman
The Gingerdead Men
Vikings Enchantress
Welcome to Scarecrow Hollow
The Pendleton Witches
The Cabinet of Curiosities
Christmas In Pine Haven
Love in the Stacks
Once Upon A Christmas
Before the Mask Falls

Dear Reader

In the pulsing darkness between midnight and dawn, where the bass beats meet bloodied streets, you've just stepped into a world where solving crimes requires more than just a badge. Welcome to "Jester Your Average Murder," where the thin blue line runs red and the nights are darker than you ever imagined.

When I first met Marissa, her story of a DJ drawn into the shadowy underbelly of supernatural crime demanded to be told. Her world—our world—is one where police procedures collide with ancient vampire hierarchies, where evidence can vanish with the rising sun, and where the most dangerous predators wear badges of their own.

This book emerged from the intersection of my fascination with both law enforcement and the eternal dance between darkness and justice. Every blood-soaked crime scene, every thundering bass drop, and every twisted revelation has been crafted to pull you deeper into this dark symphony of murder and mythology.

Thank you for daring to cross this threshold with me. As you turn these pages, remember: in this world, even the protectors cast no reflection, and sometimes the most dangerous monsters are the ones who've sworn to serve and protect.

Your guide through the darkness,

Yours in blood,

Patti

P.S. Keep your silver close and your suspicions closer.

Patti Petrone Miller

For Harold and the many nights spent at the library laughing...

The Frosted Felony

"Just finished this in one sitting and wow! I'm usually pretty good at figuring out whodunit, but this one had me guessing right up until the end. Love how the author describes all the baking - I actually tried making the lemon bars from the recipe at the back and they turned out amazing. My only complaint is now I want to bake (and eat!) everything mentioned in the book. Can't wait for the next one!"

"This is exactly what I need after a long day at work. It's like having a warm cookie and a mystery all wrapped up in one! The main character feels like someone I'd want to be friends with in real life, and I found myself laughing at her inner monologues. Some cozy mysteries can be a bit too cutesy, but this one strikes the perfect balance. Is there a book 2!"

- BookishBaker ★★★★★

Mamma Mia It's Murder

"As someone who grew up in an Italian family, I can tell you the author NAILED the family dynamics! I could practically hear my own nonna yelling about someone messing up her kitchen while I was reading this. The mystery kept me hooked, but it was the family scenes that really made me fall in love with this book. Plus, the sauce recipe included is *chef's kiss* perfection!"

- MariaC ★★★★★

"Had me staying up way too late because I HAD to know who did it! The main character reminds me so much of my best friend - stubborn but in the best way possible. Fair warning: don't read while hungry because all the food descriptions will have you raiding your kitchen at midnight. Also, the ending? Did NOT see that coming!"

MysteryLover84 ★★★★

Excerpt

"It's a trap," Sister Angelique said immediately.

"Obviously. But do we have a choice?" Mills stood, fighting back the last remnants of hunger. "He's always been one step ahead of us. Everything that's happened – Elena's death, my transformation, the brides hunting Marissa – it's all been part of his plan."

"So we spring the trap," Marissa said. "But on our terms."

"No." Mills' voice was firm. "You're not going anywhere near—"

"I'm already involved," she cut him off. "The Comte made sure of that. And like it or not, you need me. We all do."

She was right, and Mills hated it. The protective instinct warring with his hunger was complicated by another feeling he didn't want to examine too closely – something deeper than mere attraction, more primal than simple affection.

"Fine," he growled. "But we do this smart. No splitting up, no heroics." He looked at Sister Angelique. "How long until sunrise?"

"Three hours. Not enough time to prepare properly."

"Then we prepare improperly." Mills could feel his true nature stirring beneath the surface, bringing with it skills and instincts he didn't remember learning. "The Comte wants to play games? Fine. Let's show him we can play too."

A cold wind swept through the cemetery, carrying with it the distant sound of the brides' hunting song. Among the tombs, white dresses flickered like ghost lights, moving steadily closer.

They had three hours until dawn, less than twenty-four until the Comte's ritual began. Somewhere in the city, five hundred dormant vampires waited to be awakened, their buried natures ready to transform New Orleans into a kingdom of eternal night.

And Mills, the detective who'd spent his career fighting supernatural evil, was apparently one of them.

The game was reaching its climax, but the rules had changed completely. The only question was: when blood called to blood and ancient natures awoke, whose side would he really be on?

The brides' song grew louder, and somewhere in his stolen mansion, the Comte raised one final glass of blood in toast to his unwitting pawns.

The true dance was about to begin.

And not everyone would survive to see the morning.

JESTER AVERAGE MURDER

Author Social Media

https://www.facebook.com/pattipetronemiller/
https://www.pinterest.com/pattipetmiller/
https://www.instagram.com/pattipetronemiller/
https://pattipetronemillerexecutiveproducer.wordpress.com/
https://bsky.app/profile/pattipetronemiller.bsky.social
https://www.threads.net/@pattipetronemiller

Patti Petrone Miller

Chapter 1: The Night Shift

The bass thrummed through Marissa Gray's bones as she adjusted the crossfader, letting the new track blend seamlessly with the dying beats of the last. From her elevated DJ booth at Jester's Haven, she had a perfect view of the writhing crowd below – tourists and locals alike moving as one undulating mass beneath the strobing lights. The air was thick with the mingled scents of spilled bourbon, sweat, and the sweet, heavy perfume of night-blooming jasmine drifting in through the open French doors.

February in New Orleans meant the city was already deep in the grip of Carnival fever. Strings of purple, green, and gold lights crisscrossed the ceiling of the club, casting jeweled shadows across faces painted with glitter and wrapped in feathered masks. Three weeks until Fat Tuesday, and the madness was only beginning.

Marissa's fingers danced across her equipment, muscle memory born from countless nights behind the decks. The current track was building to its crescendo, and she could feel the crowd's anticipation mounting. This was her favorite part of the job – that electric moment when hundreds of strangers connected through nothing but rhythm and sound.

"Looking good up there, chère." The voice carried easily over the music, pitched just right to reach her ears. Cassie Laurent appeared at the edge of the booth, her dark curls wreathed in the purple smoke from her cigarette. Even in the dim light, her friend's honey-brown skin seemed to glow with an inner radiance that had nothing to do with the club's lighting.

"Shouldn't you be working?" Marissa called back, grinning as she cued up the next track. The witch – though most people just knew her as the club's lead bartender – shrugged one elegant shoulder.

"Taking my break. Besides, something feels off tonight." Cassie's eyes, lined with gold that matched the flecks in her irises, swept across the crowd below. The last time she'd had that look, three people had been carried out with alcohol poisoning before midnight.

Marissa learned long ago not to discount Cassie's hunches. Being born into one of New Orleans' oldest voodoo families meant her friend's "feelings" usually had substance behind them. "Bad off or weird off?"

"Can't tell yet. But—" Cassie broke off, her cigarette freezing halfway to her lips. "Well, hello there, handsome."

Following her friend's gaze, Marissa spotted him immediately. In a sea of carnival colors and exposed skin, the man stood out like a shadow at noon. Tall, broad-shouldered, wearing a charcoal suit that probably cost more than she made in two months. His face was half-hidden behind a traditional Venetian bauta mask, all sharp angles and gleaming black lacquer. Even from this distance, something about him made the hair on the back of her neck stand up.

"New money," Cassie declared, taking a long drag. "Has to be. Old money doesn't come to Jester's Haven. They stick to Bourbon Street or their private clubs."

"Speaking from experience?" Marissa teased, though her eyes stayed fixed on the stranger. He moved through the crowd like smoke, barely seeming to touch the people around him. No one appeared to notice him either, their eyes sliding past as if he wasn't there at all.

Cassie snorted. "Please. My family might be old, but we were never that kind of rich. Besides—" She stopped again, this time straightening up so fast she nearly dropped her cigarette. "Shit. We've got trouble."

Two men had just pushed through the front doors, their bearing marking them as clearly as if they'd been wearing uniforms. Cops. The taller one paused just inside the entrance, scanning the room with the practiced ease of someone who'd done it a thousand times before. Even in plainclothes, Detective Grady Mills carried authority like a second skin. Marissa was personally familiar enough to know his reputation – good cop, bad attitude, worse temper when crossed, but articulate and smart.

His partner, Detective McBride, was already making his way toward the bar. Unlike Mills, whose dark features and perpetual scowl tended to clear a path, McBride cultivated an easier presence. Tonight, he was smiling and nodding at the regulars, playing up the good cop routine.

"They're not here for a drink," Cassie muttered, crushing out her cigarette. "I better get back behind the bar before—" She cursed softly in French. "Too late."

Mills was heading straight for the DJ booth, his expression grim even behind the week-old stubble. As he drew closer, Marissa noticed something else – the shadows under his eyes were deeper than usual, his normally immaculate shirt wrinkled as if he'd been wearing it too long.

The masked stranger chose that moment to melt into the crowd, disappearing as suddenly as he'd appeared. Marissa felt a chill that had nothing to do with the air conditioning.

"Miss Gray." Mills' voice was gravel over glass, pitched to carry without shouting. "Need a word."

"What happened to Marissa? You know me well enough." Marissa checked her playlist – she had about four minutes before she needed to transition again. "Kind of in the middle of something, Detective."

"Grady." he responded in kind. "You know me well enough…" he echoed her sentiments.

"It's about Elena Martinez."

The name hit like a bucket of ice water. Elena was one of her regulars, a dancer at one of the higher-end clubs down the street. She'd been in just last night, buying rounds for everyone and talking about some fancy party she'd scored an invitation to.

"What about Elena?" Marissa asked, already dreading the answer. Mills' expression said it all.

"Found her body three hours ago. Behind St. Louis Cathedral." He paused, jaw working. "She's the third one this month."

"Jack the Ripper at it again?" she asked.

The music suddenly felt too loud, too bright, too everything. Marissa's fingers moved on autopilot, adjusting levels she didn't need to touch. "Third what?" She glanced up at him.

"Third victim with the same MO. All young women, all found in the Quarter. All—" He glanced at the crowd below, lowering his voice. "All drained of blood. Complete exsanguination, according to the Medical Examiner. And all with the same marks on their necks. Now if you ask anyone else, they might say a rabid dog...but in this case I think we know better."

Cassie made a small sound, something between a gasp and a prayer then made the sign of the cross over her body. Marissa knew what her friend was thinking – they'd both grown up on the stories, the old warnings passed down through generations of Quarter residents. Don't invite strangers into your home after dark. Line your windows with salt. And never, ever accept an invitation to a party if you don't know the host.

"Elena mentioned a party," Marissa said slowly, the pieces clicking together. "Something exclusive. She was excited about it, said some European guy had bought one of the old places on Burgundy Street and was throwing these amazing balls leading up to Mardi Gras. Said it smelled like margaritas and cotton candy and something she explained as dirt."

Mills' eyes sharpened. "Did she mention a name? The Comte de Saint-Germain?"

The temperature seemed to drop ten degrees. Even over the pounding music, Marissa could have sworn she heard Cassie whisper a ward against evil.

"Yeah, that was it. She said—" The memory surfaced, crystal clear and suddenly terrifying. "She said he was the most beautiful man she'd ever seen. That looking into his eyes was like falling into forever."

"Dammit." The word carried weight beyond its single syllable. Mills ran a hand through his dark hair, messing it up further. "That matches what the other victims' friends said. All of them attended one of the Comte's parties before they died. All of them described him the same way."

The song was ending. Marissa forced herself to focus, executing a smooth transition into the next track. The crowd below kept dancing, oblivious to the conversation happening above them. Oblivious to the fact that something evil was stalking their city, hiding behind wealth and charm and endless parties.

"The last victim," Mills continued, "Catherine Broussard. She was found two weeks ago in Jackson Square. Before that, it was Marie Dubois, left posed on a bench in Louis Armstrong Park. All three women were young, beautiful, and well-connected in the nightlife scene. All three attended different parties at the Comte's mansion. And all three—" He pulled out his phone, showing her a photo that made her stomach lurch.

The woman in the picture could have been sleeping, if not for the unnatural paleness of her skin and the twin puncture wounds on her neck. She was wearing an elaborate ball gown, her dark hair arranged artfully around her face. Someone had placed a carnival mask over her eyes – a delicate thing of silver and crystal that caught the crime scene lights like tears.

"There's more." Mills swiped to another photo. This one showed Elena's wrist, where something had been carved into the skin with surgical precision. The symbol looked like a cross between a fleur-de-lis and some kind of ancient rune.

Cassie leaned in, her breath catching. "That's old magic," she whispered. "Very old. And very dark."

Mills' eyebrows rose slightly, but he didn't comment on her expertise. Instead, he turned back to Marissa. "We need to know everything Elena told you about this party. Every detail, no matter how small. And—" He hesitated, clearly wrestling with something. "We need to know if anyone else in your circle has received an invitation."

The implications hit her like a physical blow. "You think he's not done. That he's choosing his victims ahead of time."

"I think," Mills said carefully, "that Mardi Gras is in three weeks, and the Comte has announced he's hosting the biggest ball of the season on Fat Tuesday itself. I think he's building to something, and these murders are just the beginning."

A movement in the crowd below caught Marissa's eye. The masked stranger was back, standing perfectly still in the midst of the dancing masses. As if sensing her gaze, he looked up, and for a moment, she could have sworn his eyes glowed red behind the mask.

Then someone moved between them, and he was gone again.

"One more thing," Mills added, his voice dropping even lower. "The M.E. found something strange in the victims' blood work. Some kind of compound she's never seen before. Almost like—" He stopped, looking uncomfortable.

"Like what?" Marissa prompted, though part of her didn't want to know.

"Like their blood had been changed somehow. Altered at a cellular level. And in their systems..." He shook his head. "Traces of something old. Really old. Carbon dating put it at several centuries, minimum."

Cassie muttered something in French that would have made her grandmother reach for the soap. "You're not dealing with a serial killer, Detective. You're dealing with something much worse."

"I'm dealing with a murderer," Mills corrected firmly, though Marissa noticed he didn't entirely dismiss Cassie's implication. "And I need your help to catch him before he kills again."

The music switched again, the heavy bass giving way to something slower, more hypnotic. Below, the crowd swayed like underwater plants, lost in the rhythm. How many of them, Marissa wondered, had received one of the Comte's elegant invitations? How many were already marked for death, just waiting for their turn at his deadly masquerade?

"I'll help," she heard herself say. "But I need something from you first."

Mills raised an eyebrow. "What's that?"

"The truth. All of it. What aren't you telling me about these murders?"

For a long moment, he just looked at her, his dark eyes unreadable. Finally, he nodded. "Not here. Meet me after your shift. We'll talk somewhere private."

"My place," Cassie interjected. "It's warded. And I think you're going to need someone who knows the old ways before this is over, Detective."

Before Mills could respond, a commotion erupted near the bar. McBride was waving urgently, pointing at his phone. Mills cursed under his breath.

"Another body," he said grimly. "Found in St. Roch Cemetery." He started to turn away, then paused. "Watch yourselves. And Marissa?" His eyes met hers, deadly serious. "If you get an invitation to one of those parties..."

"I won't accept it," she promised.

"You tell me…" he said with finality.

But as she watched him disappear into the crowd, Marissa couldn't shake the feeling that it might not be her choice. The masked stranger's appearance, Elena's death, the Comte's mysterious parties – it all felt connected, like pieces of a puzzle she couldn't quite see.

The night pressed against the windows of Jester's Haven, thick and heavy with secrets. Somewhere out there, an ancient evil was preparing for the grandest celebration New Orleans had seen in centuries. And somehow, Marissa knew she was already part of his deadly game.

The music played on, but suddenly every shadow held the possibility of fanged smiles and glowing eyes. Mardi Gras was coming, and with it, a darkness older than the city itself.

In the crowd below, a woman in a golden mask raised her glass in Marissa's direction. The gesture might have seemed friendly, if not for the familiar symbol glinting on her wrist – the same symbol carved into Elena's flesh.

The game was already beginning. And Marissa had just become a player, whether she wanted to be or not.

The clock struck midnight, and somewhere in the French Quarter, someone started to scream.

Chapter 2: The Witching Hour

Dawn was still hours away when Marissa followed Cassie through the wrought-iron gates of her friend's townhouse. The building was typical of the neighborhood – narrow, three stories tall, with a facade of weathered brick and shutters painted a deep purple that looked black in the darkness. Banana leaves rustled in the courtyard, and somewhere, wind chimes made of bone and crystal sang a discordant lullaby.

The screams they'd heard earlier had come from a homeless man who'd discovered victim number four propped against a tomb in St. Roch Cemetery. By the time Mills and McBride arrived, a crowd had gathered, held back by a thin line of uniformed officers. Marissa had watched the scene unfold through the traffic cameras she'd pulled up on her phone, her set at Jester's Haven running on autopilot while her thoughts swirled with endless scenarios, each worse than the last.

"Protection salt," Cassie murmured now, scuffing her boot through a line of white crystals that crossed the threshold. "Need to refresh it tomorrow. The energy's been wrong lately, like something's testing the boundaries."

The interior of the house was a study in organized chaos. Dried herbs hung from the ceiling in neat bundles, filling the air with a complex mixture of sage, rosemary, and things Marissa couldn't name. Shelves lined every wall, crammed with books whose spines bore titles in languages she didn't recognize. A massive black cat sprawled across an antique fainting couch, opening one golden eye to assess them before going back to sleep.

"Baron's in a mood," Cassie noted, dropping her keys in a bowl by the door. The bowl sat on a table whose surface was carved with symbols similar to the one found on Elena's wrist. "He always gets like this when death magic's in the air."

Marissa had long ago stopped questioning the fact that her best friend named her cats after loa. It was just one of those things that came with being friends with a daughter of New Orleans' most prominent voodoo family.

"Mills should be here soon," she said, checking her phone. No messages, but there was an email from an address she didn't recognize. The subject line was in French: *Une Invitation à Danser, ("An Invitation to Dance.")* Her finger hovered over it for a moment before she closed the app. That was a problem for later.

Cassie was already moving through the house, lighting candles and muttering incantations under her breath. The flames sparked different colors – blue, green, purple – casting strange shadows on the walls. "We need to be ready. If what I think is happening is actually happening..." She trailed off, disappearing into what she called her workroom.

Marissa sank onto a chair that wasn't occupied by books or magical paraphernalia, suddenly aware of how long she'd been on her feet. The events of the night played through her mind like a broken record: the masked stranger, Elena's death, the symbol, the fourth victim found before they could even process the third. And now an email that could only be from one source.

"Here." Cassie reappeared, pressing a mug of something hot into her hands. Steam rose from the surface, smelling of honey and herbs and something deeper, more primal. "For protection. And clarity."

The liquid burned going down, but left behind a sensation of warmth and sharp awareness. Marissa's exhaustion faded, replaced by a heightened perception that made every shadow seem significant, every sound laden with meaning.

A knock at the door made them both jump. Baron lifted his head, hissing softly.

"It's Mills," Cassie said, though Marissa noticed she checked the security sigils by the door before opening it. "And... interesting."

Detective Grady Mills stood on the porch, his shirt now sporting what looked like cemetery dirt and something darker. Behind him, looking distinctly uncomfortable, was his partner McBride. And between them...

"Sister Angelique," Cassie breathed, dropping into a respectful curtsy that looked completely natural despite her ripped jeans and combat boots.

The woman who swept into the house moved like smoke on water, her white dress seemingly untouched by the French Quarter's perpetual grime. Her dark skin was lined with age and wisdom, her white hair wrapped in an intricate tignon that incorporated feathers and bones. But it was her eyes that held Marissa's attention – they were the color of honey held up to sunlight, and they seemed to see straight through to her soul.

"Child of Laurent," Sister Angelique acknowledged Cassie with a slight nod. "Your grandmother sends her regards. And her warnings." Her gaze shifted to Marissa. "The DJ from Jester's Haven. Yes, you'll do nicely."

"Do nicely for what?" Mills asked sharply. There was tension in his stance, the kind that came from seeing too many things that didn't fit into a rational worldview.

Sister Angelique smiled, revealing teeth that seemed just a bit too sharp. "For saving your city, Detective. Or helping to, at least." She settled onto the fainting couch, and Baron immediately crawled into her lap, purring like a motor boat. "Tell me what you know of the Comte de Saint-Germain."

Mills and McBride exchanged looks before Mills spoke. "Wealthy European, bought the old Delavigne mansion on Burgundy two months ago. Started throwing elaborate parties almost immediately. No one seems to know where his money comes from, and his paperwork is perfect. Too perfect."

"Because it's all forgery," Sister Angelique said calmly, stroking Baron's fur. "Very good forgery, mind you. The kind that only centuries of practice can produce."

McBride made a sound of disbelief, but Mills just watched the old woman with intense focus. "The blood work from the victims," he said slowly. "The compound the ME couldn't identify, and the traces of something centuries old..."

"Vampire blood," Sister Angelique confirmed. "Very old vampire blood. The Comte is one of the Originals – the first of his kind, turned in the courts of Europe when magic still walked openly in the world. He's been to New Orleans before, though few remember. In 1837, just before the great fever epidemic. And before that, in 1763, during the transition from French to Spanish rule."

Marissa's hand went to her phone, where that email waited unopened. "The parties," she said. "They're hunting grounds."

"Yes and no." Sister Angelique's eyes gleamed in the candlelight. "The deaths are ritual. Each victim chosen for specific qualities, their blood taken in a precise way at a precise time. The Comte is building to something. Something that can only be accomplished during Carnival, when the veil between worlds is thinnest and the city's energy is at its peak."

McBride finally found his voice. "This is insane. You're talking about vampires and magic like they're real. Like—"

"Like the symbol carved into Elena Martinez's wrist?" Cassie interrupted. She'd been drawing something in a leather-bound book, and now she held it up. The symbol matched exactly, but around it she'd added annotations in what looked like ancient French. "This is old magic, Detective. Blood magic. Each victim is a point in a pattern, their deaths forming a sigil across the city itself."

"A sigil for what?" Mills demanded.

Sister Angelique's expression grew grave. "For opening a door. The Comte seeks to thin the barriers between life and death, to bring something through from the other side. Something that should have stayed buried centuries ago."

The candles flickered, though there was no breeze. In the distance, church bells began to toll, marking the hour before dawn.

"The invitation," Marissa said suddenly. "I received an email tonight. 'Une Invitation à Danser.' It has to be from him."

The temperature in the room seemed to drop. Sister Angelique sat forward, disturbing Baron, who leapt to the floor with an irritated yowl. "Open it. Now."

With trembling fingers, Marissa pulled up her email. The message was brief, written in elegant script:

Mademoiselle Gray,

Your reputation precedes you. The music you create, the energy you channel – it has not gone unnoticed. I would be honored if you would attend a small gathering at my home this coming Friday evening. A select group of New Orleans' most talented individuals will be in attendance.

The dress code is formal. Masks are, of course, required.

Yours most sincerely, Le Comte de Saint-Germain

"Friday," Mills muttered. "That's only three days away."

"The new moon," Cassie and Sister Angelique said in unison.

"She can't go," Mills stated flatly. "It's too dangerous. We'll find another way to—"

"She must go," Sister Angelique cut him off. "This is no coincidence. The Comte chose her specifically, just as he chose the others. But unlike them, she has protection." She pointed to the mug Cassie had given Marissa. "The Laurent family's sight-clearing brew. And now, my presence here. The spirits themselves have aligned to put these pieces in place."

"I'll go with her," Mills insisted. "Undercover."

Sister Angelique's laugh was like wind through dry leaves. "You cannot simply walk into the Comte's domain uninvited, Detective. But..." She studied him thoughtfully. "There may be a way. Though it will require sacrifice. And trust."

"What kind of sacrifice?" Mills asked warily.

Before Sister Angelique could answer, all the candles in the room guttered simultaneously. Baron arched his back, hissing at something only he could see. And through the front windows came the sound of singing – beautiful, ethereal, and somehow wrong.

Cassie was at the window in an instant, peering through a gap in the curtains. "There's someone out there. A woman in white, just standing in the middle of the street."

Marissa joined her friend at the window. The female figure was pale as moonlight, her dress moving in a wind that didn't touch anything else. As they watched, she turned her head toward the house, revealing a face that was inhumanly beautiful – and completely, utterly dead.

"One of his brides," Sister Angelique said grimly. "He knows we're gathering forces against him. This is a warning."

The woman in the street opened her mouth, and the singing grew louder. It was entrancing, compelling, making Marissa want to open the door and walk out to her...

"Don't listen!" Cassie's voice seemed to come from far away. She was running through the house, throwing handfuls of something that smelled like graveyard dirt and roses. "Cover your ears!"

But it was too late. The singing had wormed its way into Marissa's brain, painting pictures of endless parties and eternal youth, of dancing until the world ended and beginning again in darkness...

The last thing she saw before consciousness fled was Mills catching her as she fell, his face twisted with concern and something else – recognition. As if he'd seen this before, as if he knew more than he was telling.

Then darkness took her, and she dreamed of masked figures dancing through streets paved with blood, while above them all, the Comte watched from his balcony, his ancient eyes gleaming with triumph.

In her dream, he turned to her and smiled, revealing fangs that dripped with golden light. "Welcome to my city, little DJ," he said in a voice like silk over steel. "The real party is about to begin."

And in the real world, as Cassie and Sister Angelique worked frantically to break the vampire's spell, a new invitation appeared in Marissa's email. This one was different – personal, pointed, and addressed not just to her, but to the detective who still held her unconscious form.

To the DJ and the Detective,

Did you think I wouldn't notice your little gathering? Your pitiful attempts at protection? Come to my ball on Friday. Both of you. Let us drop these pretenses and play our game openly.

After all, Carnival is a time for masks... but some secrets cannot stay hidden forever.

Yours eternally, Le Comte

The night grew darker, and somewhere in the French Quarter, ancient evil stirred in its stolen mansion, counting down the hours until the next phase of its centuries-old plan could begin.

Dawn was coming, but for the first time in living memory, its arrival felt more like a threat than a promise.

Chapter 3: Shadows of the Past

Marissa woke to the taste of copper and roses on her tongue. She was lying on Cassie's fainting couch, a heavy quilt made of African symbols and New Orleans charms draped over her. Pale morning light filtered through the windows, bringing with it the sounds of a French Quarter morning – street sweepers, early tourists, and the distant toll of St. Louis Cathedral's bells.

"Drink this." Mills appeared at her side, holding a cup that smelled of coffee and something sharper. His shirt was completely ruined now, stained with a mixture of cemetery dirt, candle wax, and what looked suspiciously like blood. "Sister Angelique says it will help clear the last of the glamour."

The liquid burned worse than Cassie's protection brew, but it chased away the lingering echoes of that haunting song. Marissa's head cleared, memories of the night rushing back with crystal clarity. "The woman in white—"

"Gone with the sunrise," Mills confirmed, settling into a nearby chair. He looked exhausted, shadows under his eyes suggesting he hadn't slept at all. "But not before delivering her message."

"The email." Marissa reached for her phone, but Mills caught her wrist.

"Already handled. McBride's running traces on the IP address, not that it'll lead anywhere. Sister Angelique says creatures like the Comte don't exactly rely on normal internet providers."

His hand was warm against her skin, callused from years of police work. Marissa noticed he didn't immediately let go, his thumb absently tracing the spot where her pulse beat steadily. If he noticed what he was doing, he gave no sign.

"Where are the others?" she asked, trying to ignore the way her heart had sped up slightly.

"McBride's at the station, running background on every death that matches our victims' profile going back fifty years. Cassie's in her workroom with Sister Angelique, doing something that involves a lot of smoke and languages I don't recognize." He finally released her wrist, running a hand through his disheveled hair. "And I'm supposed to be keeping an eye on you in case there are any... aftereffects."

The way he hesitated on the last word caught her attention. "You've seen this before, haven't you? The singing, the glamour, all of it."

Mills was silent for a long moment, his dark eyes fixed on something only he could see. When he spoke, his voice was rougher than usual. "Five years ago, there was a case. String of disappearances along the Gulf Coast, all young women involved in the music scene. Singers, mostly. We tracked the perpetrator to a compound outside Baton Rouge. What we found there..." He stopped, jaw working. "The official report says we broke up a human trafficking ring. The unofficial version..."

"Tell me," Marissa urged softly.

"The place was like something out of a nightmare. Underground chambers filled with women in white dresses, all of them singing that same song. Their eyes were completely blank, like there was nothing left inside. And in the center of it all, there was this man. Beautiful, they said later. Hypnotic. But all I remember are his eyes – ancient and hungry and completely inhuman."

"What happened?"

"Official story? Suspect resisted arrest, died in the confrontation. Building caught fire, total loss. The women were taken to hospitals, but none of them remembered anything." His hands clenched into fists. "Unofficial story? The thing we were hunting wasn't human. It took three clips of blessed silver bullets to bring it down, and even then, it was laughing as it burned. Called me by name. Said we'd meet again when 'the time was right.'"

A chill ran through Marissa despite the morning warmth. "You think it was the Comte?"

"No. One of his kind, maybe, but not him. Sister Angelique says the Comte's different. Older. More powerful." Mills finally met her eyes. "Which is why you're not going to that ball."

"Pretty sure that's not your decision to make, Detective."

"Damn it, Marissa! I've seen what these creatures do to people. How they play with their food before they feed. I'm not letting—"

"Letting me what?" She sat up straighter, ignoring the way the room spun slightly. "Risk my life? News flash, Detective – it's already at risk. The Comte invited me specifically, which means I'm already on his radar. And if Sister Angelique is right about him building to some kind of ritual, we need to know what he's planning."

"She's right." Cassie's voice came from the doorway. She looked drained, her usual vibrant energy dimmed by whatever magical workings she'd been doing. "The cards are clear. Marissa has to go to that ball, and you have to go with her."

Mills started to protest, but Cassie held up a hand. "Sister Angelique found a way. Old magic, dangerous but effective. It'll let you enter the Comte's domain without an official invitation, but there's a price."

"There always is," Mills muttered.

"Blood calls to blood," Sister Angelique said, gliding into the room like a ghost in white linen. "The Comte's power flows through the victims' veins, changing them. To enter his domain uninvited, you must take that power into yourself. Become, temporarily, what he is."

The implications hit Marissa like a physical blow. "You want to turn Mills into a vampire?"

"A half-turn," Sister Angelique corrected. "Temporary, lasting only until sunrise after the ball. But yes, Detective Mills would need to drink the blood of one of the victims. Mixed with certain elements, prepared under the dark of the moon, it would grant him enough of the Comte's essence to pass the mansion's wards."

Mills had gone very still. "And the side effects?"

"Increased strength, enhanced senses. A certain... sensitivity to sunlight, though not the full vulnerability of true vampires. And hunger." Sister Angelique's honey-colored eyes were unblinking. "You would need to feed at least once before the ball. Animal blood would suffice."

"Jesus Christ." Mills stood abruptly, pacing the length of the room. "This is insane. All of it. I'm a cop, not some... supernatural detective."

"You've been both for longer than you admit," Sister Angelique said quietly. "Why do you think you were assigned to the Quarter? Why your superiors look the other way when your reports mention things that don't quite add up? New Orleans has always needed guardians who walk in both worlds, Detective Mills. It's time you embraced that role."

Before Mills could respond, Marissa's phone chimed. Another email, this one containing only an image – a photograph of her leaving Jester's Haven the night before, taken from across the street. In it, she was looking directly at the camera, though she had no memory of seeing anyone there. Her eyes in the photo were strange, reflecting light like a cat's.

"He's watching," Cassie breathed, looking over her shoulder. "Has been all along."

"The ball is in three days," Sister Angelique said. "The ritual must be performed tonight, under the dark moon, if Detective Mills is to be ready in time." She produced a small velvet bag from somewhere in her voluminous skirts. "I've brought what we need. The choice, however, must be his."

Mills had stopped pacing, his expression unreadable. "If I don't do this, you'll go to that ball alone," he said to Marissa. It wasn't a question.

"Yes."

"Even knowing what he is? What he does to his victims?"

Marissa met his gaze steadily. "Especially knowing that. Someone has to stop him, Detective. And like it or not, I'm already part of this."

The tension in the room was thick enough to cut. Finally, Mills nodded once, sharply. "What do you need me to do?"

Sister Angelique's smile was all teeth. "First, we prepare the space. Then, Detective, you learn what it means to hunt in the dark."

The next few hours passed in a blur of preparation. Cassie and Sister Angelique transformed the workroom into something ancient and primal, drawing symbols on the floors and walls with mixtures of ash, blood, and herbs that filled the air with heavy, intoxicating scents. Candles burned with black flames at precise points around the room, and in the center, they placed a silver chalice containing a mixture Marissa decided she was better off not examining too closely.

As the sun began to set, Sister Angelique drew Mills into the center of the elaborate pattern they'd created. He'd removed his ruined shirt, and Marissa tried not to stare at the scars that crossed his torso – some from his police work, others that looked much, much older.

"Last chance to back out," he said, though his tone suggested he already knew her answer.

"Not a chance, Detective." She managed a smile. "Besides, someone needs to make sure you don't go full vampire and start wearing capes."

His answering laugh was strained but genuine. Then Sister Angelique began to chant, and there was no more time for banter.

The ritual itself was both more and less dramatic than Marissa expected. No thunderbolts or dramatic winds, just a gradual deepening of shadows and a sensation of pressure building in her ears. Mills drank from the chalice when instructed, his face twisting at the taste. For a moment, nothing seemed to happen.

Then he screamed.

The sound was unlike anything Marissa had ever heard – pure agony mixed with something darker, hungrier. Mills fell to his knees, his body convulsing as the changes took hold. Veins stood out black against his skin, pulsing with power that wasn't meant for mortal flesh.

Marissa started forward, but Cassie held her back. "Don't," her friend warned. "The circle has to hold."

The transformation seemed to last forever, though Sister Angelique had assured them it would only be minutes. When it was finally over, Mills lay gasping in the center of the circle, his body sheened with sweat.

Slowly, he raised his head. His eyes, when they met Marissa's, were different – still dark, but with a predatory gleam that hadn't been there before. When he spoke, his voice was rougher, and she caught a glimpse of newly elongated canines.

"Well," he said with grim humor, "that's one way to get into a party."

Sister Angelique broke the circle with a wave of her hand. "How do you feel?"

"Hungry." The word came out like a growl. "And... everything's different. Sharper. I can hear your heartbeats, smell your blood..." He stopped, visibly forcing back the hunger. "How long until this becomes permanent?"

"Sunrise after the ball," Sister Angelique assured him. "Unless you feed on human blood before then. That would complete the transformation, make it irreversible."

"Noted." Mills stood carefully, testing his new balance. His movements were different now – more fluid, predatory. "What's next?"

"Now," Cassie said, "we teach you to control it. Before you can play at being a vampire at the Comte's ball, you need to learn how they move, how they think." She glanced at Sister Angelique. "And we need to get you fed before the hunger drives you mad."

"I'll handle that part," Sister Angelique said. "Miss Gray, you should return home. Rest. Prepare for what's coming." Her honey-colored eyes seemed to see straight through to Marissa's soul. "The Comte will be watching you more closely now. Dreams are his favorite hunting ground."

As if on cue, Marissa's phone chimed again. Another email, this one containing a video attachment. With trembling fingers, she pressed play.

The footage showed the interior of what had to be the Comte's mansion, filmed during one of his infamous parties. Masked figures whirled in elaborate dances, their movements just a little too perfect to be human. And there, holding court from a balcony overlooking the ballroom, was a figure she recognized – the masked stranger from Jester's Haven.

The camera zoomed in on his face as he turned, looking directly into the lens. Slowly, deliberately, he removed his mask, revealing features of such ethereal beauty they almost hurt to look at. But it was his eyes that held her attention – ancient, hungry, and filled with a terrible knowledge.

His lips moved, forming words meant only for her: "I look forward to our dance, little DJ."

The video ended, leaving Marissa with a certainty that chilled her to her bones. The Comte hadn't just invited her to his ball.

He'd been watching her all along, orchestrating every move in this deadly game. And now, with Mills transformed and the pieces all in place, the real dance was about to begin.

In three days, she would enter the lion's den with a half-turned vampire as her only protection. And somewhere in that mansion of horrors and ancient evil, the answer to what the Comte was planning waited to be discovered.

Assuming, of course, they survived long enough to find it.

The sun set over New Orleans, painting the sky in colors that reminded Marissa too much of blood. And in the growing darkness, Mills' new eyes gleamed with a hunger that was both terrible and fascinating.

The game was changing, the stakes rising with every passing hour. And somewhere in his stolen mansion, the Comte raised a glass of something that definitely wasn't wine, toasting the next phase of his centuries-old plan.

The clock was ticking, and Mardi Gras was coming. But first, they had a ball to attend.

Chapter 4: Blood and Bourbon

The hunger was unbearable.

Mills stood in the shadows of Lafayette Cemetery, every sense hyperaware of the life pulsing around him. He could hear heartbeats from half a block away, smell the copper-sweet scent of blood beneath warm skin. Even the rats scurrying between the tombs called to his new instincts, promising relief from the gnawing emptiness inside him.

"Focus," Sister Angelique commanded. She stood nearby, her white dress gleaming like a ghost in the darkness. A cooler sat at her feet, and Mills tried not to think about what it contained. "Control the hunger, don't let it control you."

"Easy for you to say," he growled. His voice sounded wrong to his enhanced hearing – too rough, too animal. "You're not the one who feels like their insides are trying to eat themselves."

"No," she agreed calmly. "I merely spent forty years helping newly turned vampires learn to manage their urges without slaughtering half the French Quarter." She kicked the cooler toward him. "Drink. Animal blood isn't as satisfying, but it will take the edge off."

Mills had done many things in his career as a detective. He'd seen the worst humanity had to offer, dealt with creatures that shouldn't exist outside of nightmares. But nothing had prepared him for this – for the way his hands shook as he opened the cooler, for the immediate response of his body to the scent of cold blood.

The first bag – pig's blood, according to the label – burst in his too-tight grip, splattering his chest and face. The second he managed to drink properly, though the plastic felt wrong against his new fangs. The taste was simultaneously revolting and the most delicious thing he'd ever experienced.

"Better?" Sister Angelique asked when he'd finished three bags.

Mills wiped his mouth, grimacing at the sticky residue on his hand. "The hunger's still there, but... manageable." He could think clearly now, at least. The sound of distant heartbeats had faded to a dull background rhythm instead of an all-consuming temptation.

"Good. Because we have company."

Marissa emerged from behind a nearby tomb, and Mills had to forcibly suppress a surge of predatory interest. She smelled like night-blooming jasmine and something deeper, more primal – power, he realized. The protection spells Cassie had woven around her gave her aura a distinct magical signature.

"You look..." She trailed off, taking in his blood-stained appearance.

"Like a horror movie extra?" He tried to smile, then remembered his fangs and stopped.

"I was going to say 'different.'" She moved closer, studying him with an intensity that made him want to either step back or move much, much closer. "Your eyes are definitely not human anymore."

"Neither is the rest of him, temporarily at least," Sister Angelique interjected. "How did your meeting with the Laurent girl go?"

Marissa held up a small velvet bag that clinked softly. "Cassie finished the protection charms. Seven total – one for each night leading up to the ball, plus extras in case something goes wrong." She glanced at Mills. "She said to tell you she's working on something to help with the sunlight issue, but it's going to take time."

The mention of sunlight made Mills' skin crawl. He'd discovered that particular aspect of his transformation the hard way earlier, when a stray beam through Sister Angelique's window had left an angry burn on his arm. It had healed within minutes, but the memory of that searing pain lingered.

"Time is something we don't have much of," Sister Angelique said grimly. She produced a newspaper from somewhere in her voluminous skirts. The headline made Mills' newly enhanced vision sharpen with predatory focus:

FIFTH VICTIM FOUND IN FRENCH QUARTER
Police Remain Silent on Possible Serial Killer

"They found her an hour ago," Marissa said quietly. "Behind Lafitte's Blacksmith Shop. Same MO as the others – completely drained, with the symbol carved into her wrist. But this time..." She hesitated, looking sick.

"This time he left a message," Mills finished. He'd gotten the call from McBride just before sunset, but hadn't been able to respond. Not while the transformation was still working through his system. "Carved into her chest, right? In French?"

Marissa nodded. "*Le temps presse, mes amis. The clock is ticking, my friends.*"

"He's accelerating his timeline." Sister Angelique's honey-colored eyes seemed to glow in the darkness. "The victims were supposed to be spaced out, one every few days leading up to Fat Tuesday. But now..."

"Now he's killing them faster," Mills said. "Why?"

"Because something's changed. Or someone has interfered with his plans." She gave Mills a pointed look. "Your transformation didn't go unnoticed, Detective. The old powers of the city felt it. Which means the Comte did too."

A new scent caught Mills' attention – fear, sharp and metallic, coming from Marissa. He turned to her, nostrils flaring. "What aren't you telling us?"

She pulled out her phone, hands shaking slightly. "I got another email. Just before I came here." She pulled up the message, and Mills had to fight back a snarl at what he saw.

The image showed Marissa sleeping in her apartment, taken through her bedroom window. But it was the figure standing over her bed that made his blood run cold – the woman in white from the night before, her dead eyes fixed on the camera as if she knew exactly who would be viewing the photo.

The message below was simple: *Sweet dreams, little DJ. Soon you'll join our dance eternal.*

"They were in my apartment," Marissa whispered. "While I was sleeping. I never even knew..."

Mills moved without thinking, covering the distance between them in a blur of inhuman speed. His hand cupped her face, tilting it up to meet his gaze. "Pack a bag. You're not staying there anymore."

"She can't stay with you," Sister Angelique pointed out. "Not while you're like this. The hunger—"

"She'll stay with me," a new voice interrupted. Cassie emerged from the shadows, looking exhausted but determined. "My wards are strongest at night anyway. And I've added some new ones, specifically keyed to keep out the dead."

Mills realized he was still touching Marissa's face and forced himself to step back. Her skin had been so warm, her pulse a siren song under his fingers...

"Detective?" Sister Angelique's voice held a warning note. "Perhaps you should have another bag from the cooler."

He nodded stiffly, trying to ignore the way Marissa's scent lingered on his skin. The animal blood was disgusting, but it helped quiet the darker urges prowling through his mind.

"We need to talk about what happens at the ball," Cassie said once he'd finished feeding. She pulled out a weathered leather notebook covered in mystical symbols.

"I've been researching the Comte's previous visits to New Orleans. In 1837, he hosted a similar series of parties during Carnival. The final ball coincided with a massive outbreak of yellow fever that killed thousands."

"And in 1763?" Marissa asked.

"The transfer of power from French to Spanish rule was marked by weeks of mysterious deaths. Bodies found drained of blood, strange symbols carved into their flesh. The historical records talk about an elegant European noble who threw elaborate parties during that time. And at his final ball..." Cassie's voice dropped. "Every guest vanished without a trace. Over three hundred people, gone in a single night."

The implications hung heavy in the cemetery air. Mills found himself moving closer to Marissa again, a protective instinct he wasn't sure came from his human side or his new vampiric nature.

"The symbols are the key," Sister Angelique said. She traced a pattern in the air, leaving trails of blue fire hanging in the darkness. "Each death is a point of power, creating a massive sigil across the city itself. But for what purpose?"

"To break down the barriers between life and death," Cassie read from her notebook. "To 'thin the veil between worlds.' That's what you said before, isn't it?"

"Yes, but—" Sister Angelique stopped suddenly, her eyes going wide. "Oh. Oh no."

"What?" Mills demanded.

"The transfer of power," she whispered. "Not just from French to Spanish rule, but from life to death itself. He's not trying to bring something through from the other side. He's trying to turn New Orleans into a city of the dead."

The words seemed to drop the temperature around them by several degrees. In the distance, church bells began to toll midnight.

"How?" Marissa asked. "How could he possibly—"

"The energy of Carnival," Cassie interrupted, her voice shaking. "All that life force, all that chaos and celebration. If he could corrupt it, turn it dark at the height of the festivities..."

"Fat Tuesday," Mills growled. "His final ball. He's going to use the guests as a massive sacrifice, channel all that death energy through the sigil he's creating with these murders."

"And with that much power," Sister Angelique finished, "he could turn the entire French Quarter into a necropolis. A city of vampires and worse things, with him as its king."

Marissa's phone chimed again. This time, the message contained a video. With trembling fingers, she pressed play.

The footage showed the interior of the Comte's mansion again, but this time the ballroom was empty save for one figure. The Comte himself stood in the center of the floor, his vampiric beauty even more striking without his mask. As they watched, he raised a crystal glass filled with something too dark to be wine.

"To new friends," he said, his voice carrying traces of centuries-old aristocratic French. "And to the coming war. The French Quarter has always been a city of masks, of secrets and shadows. Soon it will be so much more." His smile revealed fangs that gleamed like pearls. "I do hope you'll all survive to see it."

The video ended, but not before they caught a glimpse of something moving in the shadows behind him – countless pale figures in white dresses, their dead eyes fixed on the camera.

"Two days," Cassie said into the heavy silence that followed. "We have two days until the ball."

"Less than that to figure out how to stop him," Mills added. The hunger was rising again, making his voice rougher. "And I need to learn how to pass for human enough to get close to him."

"We'll need help," Sister Angelique said. "I know someone... but you're not going to like it, Detective."

"Who?"

"The vampire you killed in Baton Rouge five years ago? He had a sister. She's been living in the Quarter ever since, running a certain establishment that caters to... specialized tastes."

Mills felt his fangs extend fully at the memory of that night. "The Black Rose. I should have known Marie Delacroix was one of them."

"She hates the Comte more than she hates you," Sister Angelique pointed out. "And she knows his ways, his weaknesses. We need her knowledge."

"She'll try to kill me on sight."

"Probably," Sister Angelique agreed. "But right now, she's our best chance at understanding what we're really up against."

Marissa stepped closer to Mills, either not noticing or not caring how his eyes fixed on the pulse in her throat.

"I'll go with you. The owner of the Black Rose might hate you, but she's been trying to book me as a DJ for months. Maybe I can get us in the door at least."

"No," Mills started to say, but Sister Angelique cut him off.

"Actually, that might work. Marie appreciates talent, and she's always looking for new blood, so to speak. If we play this right..."

"I don't like it," Mills growled.

"You don't have to like it," Sister Angelique snapped. "You just have to learn enough control to get through the next forty-eight hours without killing anyone. Starting with her." She nodded toward Marissa.

The truth of those words hit Mills like a physical blow. Even now, with animal blood dulling the worst of his hunger, part of him was hyperaware of Marissa's proximity. Of her warmth, her scent, the way her blood called to his new instincts...

"Tomorrow night," he said roughly, taking several steps back. "We'll go to the Black Rose tomorrow night. Right now, I need..." He stopped, fighting back the hunger. "I need to not be around humans for a while."

Understanding filled Marissa's eyes, along with something else – not fear, exactly, but awareness. She could see the predator in him now, the monster lurking behind his human face.

"I'll take him to the old monastery," Sister Angelique said. "The wards there will help him focus, learn control." She fixed Marissa with a stern look. "You go with Cassie. Stay behind her wards. And whatever you do, don't fall asleep without the protection charms."

"Why?" Marissa asked, though she looked like she already knew the answer.

"Because the Comte isn't the only one who can walk in dreams," Sister Angelique said grimly. "And his brides are hungry."

As if in response to her words, a cold wind swept through the cemetery, carrying with it the distant sound of ethereal singing. Mills watched Marissa shiver and had to fight back the urge to go to her, to wrap her in his arms and shield her from what was coming.

But he couldn't protect her, not really. Not when part of him wanted to tear her throat out.

The hunger rose again, and with it came a terrible certainty: if they survived the next two days, it would be a miracle. If they survived with their humanity intact...

Well, that might be too much to ask for.

The moon hung low over New Orleans, casting shadows that seemed to move with purpose through the ancient cemetery. And somewhere in his mansion, the Comte raised another glass of blood, toasting the chaos to come.

The game was entering its final phase, and the stakes were higher than any of them had imagined. The question wasn't just whether they could stop him anymore.

The question was how much of themselves they'd have to sacrifice to do it.

And in the growing darkness, Mills' new instincts whispered that the answer might be: everything.

Chapter 5: The Black Rose

The Black Rose sat in the heart of the French Quarter, its elegant facade belying the true nature of what lay within. To mortal eyes, it appeared to be merely another high-end nightclub, its art deco exterior restored to Jazz Age perfection. But Mills' enhanced vision revealed the truth – sigils of power worked into the wrought iron balconies, wards etched in blood beneath the fresh paint, and shadows that moved against the flow of passing traffic.

"Ready?" Marissa stood beside him, dressed for the part in a vintage-inspired black dress that made his new instincts stir uncomfortably. The protection charms Cassie had given her were woven into an intricate choker at her throat, the crystals pulsing faintly with contained power.

"No," Mills admitted. The sun had only been down for an hour, and the hunger was already clawing at his insides despite the animal blood Sister Angelique had forced him to drink earlier. "But we're out of options."

The line outside the Black Rose wrapped around the block, an eclectic mix of tourists seeking thrills and locals who knew exactly what kind of establishment they were queuing for. The bouncer – a massive man whose heartbeat was significantly slower than human normal – nodded to them immediately.

"Miss Gray," he rumbled, unhooking the velvet rope. "Madame Delacroix is expecting you." His nostrils flared as Mills passed, and something like recognition flickered in his too-pale eyes. "Both of you."

The interior of the Black Rose was a study in controlled decadence. Crystal chandeliers cast warm light over red velvet booths and tables of dark mahogany. A jazz quartet played on a raised stage, their music carrying undertones that made Mills' new senses tingle with recognition – not quite a vampire's hunting song, but something similar.

And everywhere, there was blood.

Not openly, of course. This wasn't some crude feeding den. But Mills could smell it – in crystal glasses that looked like they held red wine, in private rooms hidden behind heavy curtains, in the slight shimmer on painted lips that had nothing to do with makeup.

"Don't look at anyone directly," he murmured to Marissa as they made their way to the bar. "Some of them can enthrall with eye contact alone."

"Noted." Her voice was steady, but he could smell the sharp edge of fear beneath her jasmine perfume. "Though I think we're the ones being watched."

She was right. The club's patrons – a mix of vampires, their human thralls, and those who sought to become either – tracked their movement with predatory interest. Mills caught whispered conversations in French, Spanish, and languages far older.

"C'est lui? The detective?"

"Newly turned, by the smell of him."

"Does Marie know he's here?"

"Oh, she knows. She knows everything that happens in her domain."

The bartender appeared before them without being summoned – a beautiful woman with caramel skin and eyes that were just slightly too green to be natural. "Madame Delacroix will see you now," she said, her Creole accent thick with age. "Through there." She nodded toward a beaded curtain that hadn't been there a moment before.

Mills let Marissa go first, fighting back the instinct to place himself between her and every vampire in the room. The corridor beyond the curtain was narrow, lined with mirrors that showed only emptiness where the vampires among the passing crowd should have been reflected.

The office at the end of the hall was everything Mills expected from a vampire queen's sanctuary – all dark woods and deeper shadows, with artifacts of power displayed like museum pieces behind glass. Marie Delacroix herself sat behind a massive desk that looked like it had been carved from a single piece of bloodwood.

She was exactly as Mills remembered from their brief encounter five years ago – ageless, elegant, with dark skin that held a slight luminescence and eyes like chips of arctic ice. She wore vintage Chanel and diamonds that sparkled with captured souls.

"Detective Mills," she said, her voice carrying centuries of aristocratic breeding. "You have considerable courage, coming to my domain after what you did to my brother."

"Your brother was kidnapping and killing innocent women," Mills growled.

"My brother was feeding according to his nature," Marie corrected. "Sloppily, perhaps, but within the ancient laws." Her cold gaze shifted to Marissa. "And you, little DJ. I've heard such interesting things about your sets at Jester's Haven. The way you weave power into your music without even realizing it."

Marissa met her gaze steadily. "We're here about the Comte."

Marie's expression didn't change, but the temperature in the room dropped several degrees. "Ah yes. The ancient one who thinks he can simply walk into my city and start changing the rules." She gestured to the chairs before her desk. "Sit. Tell me what you know."

Over the next several minutes, they laid out everything – the murders, the sigil being created across the city, the Comte's apparent plan to transform the French Quarter during his Fat Tuesday ball. Marie listened without interruption, her fingers tracing patterns on her desk that left trails of frost in their wake.

"So," she said when they finished, "the Comte seeks to create his own domain, right in the heart of mine. How... ambitious of him." Her smile showed just a hint of fang. "And you, Detective, have allowed yourself to be partially turned just to infiltrate his little soirée. That must be... difficult, with one so tempting so near."

Mills forced himself not to react as Marie's words brought his hunger surging to the surface. Beside him, Marissa's heartbeat quickened slightly.

"We need information," he said roughly. "Weaknesses, vulnerabilities. Anything we can use against him."

"Information has a price, Detective. Especially information about one of the Originals." Marie leaned forward, her cold eyes gleaming. "But first, a demonstration. To prove you can handle what I might tell you." She pressed a button on her desk. "Send in the volunteer."

A side door opened, and a young woman entered. She was beautiful in the way all vampire thralls tended to be, with pale skin and eyes that held both fear and desperate yearning. The scent of her blood hit Mills like a physical blow.

"Fresh from the source," Marie said softly. "Not that animal swill Sister Angelique has been feeding you. Show me you can feed without killing, Detective, and perhaps we can discuss terms."

"No." The word came out as a snarl. "I won't—"

"Then you'll never learn what you need to know." Marie's voice hardened. "The Comte is not some newly turned fledgling. He has powers you cannot imagine, defenses built over centuries. If you cannot even manage a simple feeding, you'll never get close enough to stop him."

The thrall moved closer, her neck bearing fresh puncture marks that made Mills' fangs extend fully. The hunger rose like a tide, threatening to drown his human consciousness.

"Mills." Marissa's voice cut through the haze of bloodlust. "Look at me."

He turned, fighting to focus on her face rather than the pulse in her throat. Her eyes held no fear now, only determination.

"You can do this," she said softly. "You're stronger than the hunger."

"Am I?" He could feel his control slipping, the predator inside him straining to break free.

"Yes." She reached out, her warm hand cupping his cold cheek. The contact sent electricity through his nervous system. "Because you have to be."

Marie watched their interaction with obvious interest. "Fascinating," she murmured. "You care for her. Even through the bloodlust, even through the hunger... you want to protect her more than you want to feed from her."

"If you're done playing games," Mills growled, "either help us or we'll leave."

"Oh, but the game is just beginning, Detective." Marie gestured, and the thrall retreated through the side door. "Very well. You've proven more interesting than I expected. I will tell you what I know of the Comte – for a price."

"Name it," Marissa said before Mills could object.

Marie's smile was terrifying in its beauty. "Three things. First, a favor to be named later, from each of you. Second, Detective Mills must spend the remainder of the night learning proper feeding techniques. If you're going to infiltrate the Comte's ball, you need to be able to pass as a natural vampire."

"And the third?" Mills asked, dreading the answer.

"The third is simple. When the time comes – and you'll know when – you must kill the Comte's newest bride. The one who's been watching your little DJ through windows and dreams."

Marissa's breath caught. "Why her specifically?"

"Because, my dear, she wasn't always one of his brides. Once, she was my daughter." Marie's icy composure cracked slightly. "The Comte took her thirty years ago, turned her into one of his white-clad abominations. I want her freed from his influence, permanently."

The implications hung heavy in the air. Mills remembered the woman in white outside Cassie's house, her beautiful dead eyes and haunting song. "You want us to destroy your own daughter?"

"I want you to release what's left of her soul," Marie corrected. "Now, do we have a deal?"

Mills looked at Marissa, seeing his own uncertainty reflected in her eyes. But what choice did they have? The ball was tomorrow night, and they were running out of options.

"Deal," he said finally. "But I want everything you know about the Comte. Every weakness, every vulnerability."

"Of course." Marie pressed another button on her desk. "Gerard will show Miss Gray to our VIP area. She can observe tonight's entertainment while you and I discuss the finer points of vampire etiquette."

"I'm not leaving her alone," Mills protested.

"She won't be alone. My people will protect her – I guarantee it." Marie's smile held no warmth. "Besides,

Detective, you need to focus. The lessons I'm about to teach you require... complete concentration."

The massive bouncer appeared in the doorway. Marissa squeezed Mills' hand once before standing. "I'll be fine," she assured him. "Learn what you need to learn."

He watched her follow Gerard out, every instinct screaming to go after her. But Marie was right – he needed to learn control, needed to understand exactly what he'd become if they were going to have any chance tomorrow night.

"Now then," Marie said once they were alone. "Let's begin with the basics of blood consumption. And while we practice, I'll tell you exactly why the Comte chose New Orleans for his great working." Her eyes gleamed with ancient malice. "After all, this isn't the first time he's tried to turn a city into his personal kingdom of the dead. It's just the first time he's had all the pieces aligned properly."

"What do you mean?"

"I mean, Detective, that everything that's happened – Elena's death, your transformation, even Miss Gray's growing involvement – it's all part of his plan. Has been from the start." She produced a crystal decanter filled with something too dark to be wine. "The question is: are you prepared to learn exactly how deep this conspiracy goes? Because I warn you, the truth will change how you see everything. Including yourself."

Mills thought of Marissa, of the way she'd looked at him with trust despite what he'd become. Of the Comte's mysterious invitation and the growing body count across the city he'd sworn to protect.

"Tell me everything," he said.

Marie's smile was a predator's warning. "Oh, I will. But first..." She opened a hidden panel in her desk, revealing a set of crystal glasses filled with fresh human blood. "Drink. You'll need your strength for what comes next."

The hunger rose again, and this time, Mills didn't fight it. They had less than twenty-four hours until the ball, and he needed every advantage he could get.

Even if those advantages came with a price his soul might not survive paying.

The night grew deeper, and somewhere above them, in the VIP area of the Black Rose, Marissa watched immortal creatures dance to music older than the city itself. And in his mansion on Burgundy Street, the Comte raised yet another glass of blood, toasting the pieces moving exactly as he'd planned.

The game was approaching its final moves, and none of them – not even Marie – knew just how high the stakes truly were.

But they were about to find out.

And the cost would be measured in blood.

Chapter 6: A Taste of Power

The VIP section of the Black Rose was a study in beautiful horror. From her velvet booth overlooking the main floor, Marissa watched immortal creatures dance and feed with equal grace. The jazz quartet had been replaced by a DJ whose equipment looked centuries old, though the sound it produced made her professional ear tingle with recognition – music designed to enthrall, to seduce, to draw prey willingly into deadly embraces.

"Your drink, mademoiselle." A server appeared silently beside her, placing a glass of deep red liquid on the table. At her alarmed look, he smiled, revealing perfectly normal teeth. "Just wine. Madame's orders – no one is to offer you anything stronger tonight."

The wine was excellent, probably worth more than she made in a month at Jester's Haven. Marissa sipped it slowly, using the glass to hide her observations of the crowd below. She recognized more faces than she'd expected – politicians, celebrities, wealthy business owners who'd always seemed just a little too ageless in their society page photos.

"Impressive, isn't it?" A woman slid into the booth across from her, moving with ethereal grace. She was stunning in that particular way all vampires seemed to be, with pale skin that somehow managed to look elegant rather than sickly, and eyes that held centuries of secrets. "The power in this room alone could run the city for a month."

"You're one of Marie's inner circle," Marissa guessed. The vampire's dress was vintage Dior, her jewelry ancient and gleaming with contained power.

"Isabelle Dumont, at your service." Her smile revealed just a hint of fang. "I knew your grandmother, you know. Remarkable woman. Her music could entrance almost as well as a vampire's song."

Marissa's hand tightened on her wine glass. "My grandmother was a jazz singer in the Quarter. Nothing more."

"Oh, child." Isabelle laughed softly. "You really don't know, do you? Why your sets at Jester's Haven affect people so strongly? Why the Comte chose you specifically?" She leaned forward, her ancient eyes gleaming. "Your grandmother wasn't just a singer. She was a siren."

The word seemed to drop the temperature around their booth by several degrees. "That's not possible. Sirens are—"

"Myth? Legend? Like vampires?" Isabelle's smile widened. "Your grandmother had a particular gift for making people... susceptible to suggestion through her music. Sound familiar?"

It did. Too familiar. Marissa thought of the way crowds at Jester's Haven moved like one organism when she played, how certain combinations of beats and rhythms could affect the entire room's energy.

"That's just good DJing," she protested weakly.

"Is it?" Isabelle gestured to the dance floor below, where the current DJ's music had the crowd moving in patterns that seemed almost ritualistic. "Watch carefully. See how he weaves the sound, how it affects their minds and bodies? That's power, dear. Raw and ancient. Just like what flows through your veins."

Before Marissa could respond, a commotion near the main entrance drew their attention. The crowd parted like water as three figures entered the Black Rose – two women in elaborate Victorian dresses and a man who could only be one person.

"The Comte," Isabelle breathed, a hint of fear coloring her voice. "He never comes here. This is Marie's territory."

The Comte was even more beautiful in person than he had been in the video, his features holding that particular quality of perfection that went beyond human genetics. He moved through the crowd like smoke, his ancient eyes scanning the room until they found Marissa.

His smile made her blood run cold.

"Now that's interesting," Isabelle murmured. "He's not supposed to be able to sense you through Marie's wards. Unless..." She cursed softly in French. "The dreams. When his bride visited you in your sleep – that created a connection."

The Comte was making his way toward the stairs that led to the VIP section. His companions – two of his white-clad brides – followed in perfect synchronization, their dead eyes fixed straight ahead.

"Back door," Isabelle said urgently. "Now. I'll delay him."

Marissa didn't need to be told twice. She slipped out of the booth and through a hidden door she hadn't noticed before, emerging into a narrow corridor lined with more spelled mirrors. Behind her, she could hear the Comte's voice – beautiful and terrible, like silk over razor blades.

"Isabelle, my dear. Still serving the usurper queen, I see?"

"My lord Comte. This is... unexpected."

"Is it? When such a unique talent graces your establishment?"

Marissa ran faster, her heels clicking on the ancient floorboards. The corridor seemed to stretch endlessly, the spelled mirrors showing disturbing reflections – herself with fangs, with dead white eyes, with blood running down her chin...

She burst through another door and found herself in what had to be Marie's private library. Floor-to-ceiling shelves held books bound in materials she didn't want to identify. Display cases contained artifacts of obvious power – a crystal skull that seemed to watch her movements, a dagger whose blade was darker than black, a music box that emanated a feeling of absolute dread.

"Beautiful, aren't they?" The Comte's voice came from behind her. He stood in the doorway she'd just come through, looking even more immortally perfect up close. "The tools and toys of our kind. Would you like to learn their secrets?"

"Stay back." Marissa's hand went to the protection charms at her throat, but they felt weak, drained.

"Those trinkets cannot protect you from me, little siren." He moved closer, his movements hypnotic. "I am older than the magic that made them. Older than this city, older than the very concept of protection spells." His smile was breathtaking in its beauty and horror. "Would you like to know why I chose you?"

"Because of my grandmother? Because I have siren blood?"

He laughed, the sound like crystal breaking. "Oh no, my dear. Because you have something far more valuable – the potential to become something entirely new. A vampire with siren abilities... imagine the possibilities."

"I'm not interested in becoming anything."

"No?" He was closer now, though she hadn't seen him move. "Not even to save your detective? Poor Mills, fighting so hard against his new nature. What if I told you there was a way to help him control the hunger? To let him keep some of his humanity?"

Marissa's back hit one of the display cases. The crystal skull inside seemed to grin at her predicament. "You're lying."

"I never lie, little siren. It's so much more entertaining to tell terrible truths." The Comte reached out, his cold fingers brushing her cheek. "Your blood, properly mutated, could save him. Could give him control over what he's becoming. All you have to do is accept my gift."

"Get away from her." Mills' voice cracked like a whip from the library's other entrance. He stood with Marie Delacroix, both of them radiating deadly intent. Blood stained his shirt collar – evidence of whatever lessons Marie had been teaching him.

The Comte didn't move his hand from Marissa's face. "Ah, the detective himself. Perfect timing. We were just discussing your... condition."

"I said, get away from her." Mills took a step forward, his eyes blazing with predatory light.

"Or what?" The Comte's smile was almost gentle. "You'll try to hurt me with your borrowed power? Your temporary fangs?" His ancient eyes locked onto Marissa's. "Ask him how many he fed from tonight, little siren. Ask him how much he enjoyed it."

"Enough." Marie's voice carried centuries of command. "You forget yourself, Comte. This is my domain."

"For now." He finally stepped back from Marissa, though his cold touch seemed to linger. "But tomorrow night, at my ball... everything changes. The board is set, the pieces in motion." His gaze swept over all of them. "I look forward to seeing you all there. Especially you, little siren. Save a dance for me."

He vanished between one blink and the next. In the display case, the crystal skull's grin seemed to widen.

"Are you alright?" Mills was at her side instantly, his enhanced speed almost matching the Comte's. This close, she could smell blood on his breath, see the way his pupils were dilated with borrowed power.

"I'm fine. But Mills... what did he mean about feeding?"

"Later," Marie interrupted. "Right now, we need to move. The Comte's appearance changes everything." She began pulling books from the shelves apparently at random. "The ritual he's planning... it's worse than we thought."

"How could it be worse than turning the city into a necropolis?" Marissa asked.

"Because that's not his real goal." Marie's cold eyes held genuine fear. "The necropolis is just a side effect. What he's really trying to do..." She stopped, holding up an ancient tome whose cover appeared to be made of mortal skin. "Here. This is what he's attempting. And if he succeeds, New Orleans will be the least of our problems."

The book fell open to a page covered in symbols similar to the ones carved into Elena's wrist. But these were larger, more complex, forming a pattern that hurt Marissa's eyes to look at.

"Mother of God," Mills breathed, his heightened vision apparently letting him read the ancient text. "He's not just trying to transform the city. He's trying to—"

A scream cut through the air – high, otherworldly, and filled with a power that shattered every mirror in the library. Through the broken glass, Marissa caught glimpses of movement – white dresses, dead eyes, hungry smiles...

The brides had found them.

And somewhere in the French Quarter, as midnight approached and disaster loomed, the Comte raised one final glass in toast to his unwitting pawns. Tomorrow night would bring his greatest triumph, and not even a half-turned detective and a fledgling siren could stop what was coming.

The end game was approaching, and the stakes were higher than any of them had imagined.

The only question was: who would survive to see what New Orleans became when the music finally stopped?

Chapter 7: Blood Ties

The brides' screams shattered more than mirrors. The sound pierced through flesh and bone, making Marissa's vision blur with supernatural power. Mills moved instantly, placing himself between her and the approaching threat, his borrowed vampire strength humming with deadly intent.

"The back passage," Marie commanded, already pulling books from shelves seemingly at random. "Behind the skull display. It leads to the catacombs."

"Catacombs?" Marissa hadn't known New Orleans had any.

"The old city lies beneath the new," Marie said cryptically. "Places where even vampires fear to tread. Now go!"

The crystal skull's display case swung open at Marie's touch, revealing a narrow stone staircase descending into darkness. The screams grew closer, accompanied by the sound of shattering glass and splintering wood.

Mills grabbed Marissa's hand, his skin cold but his grip gentle despite his strength. "Stay close."

They plunged into the darkness just as the library doors burst inward. Through the closing passage, Marissa caught a glimpse of white dresses and dead eyes, of Marie raising her hands as frost spread across the floor and walls.

The stairs seemed to descend forever, the air growing thick with age and secrets. Mills navigated the darkness easily with his vampire sight, but Marissa had to rely on his guidance and the faint glow of her protection charms.

"The Comte was lying," she said finally, breaking the tense silence. "About being able to help you control the hunger."

Mills' grip on her hand tightened slightly. "I know." His voice was rough, and she could hear the strain of controlling his predatory instincts. "But that's not what worries me. What he said about your blood, about you becoming something new..."

"A vampire with siren abilities," she quoted. "But I'm not—"

"You are." He stopped suddenly, turning to face her in the darkness. His eyes glowed faintly, reflecting what little light reached them. "I can smell it in your blood. The power. It's what drew me to you even before all this, though I didn't understand why."

The confession hung between them, heavy with implications. Before Marissa could respond, a distant scream echoed through the catacombs – closer than it should have been possible.

"They're in the tunnels," Mills growled. "We need to move."

The passage opened into a larger chamber that might once have been a wine cellar. Ancient bottles lined the walls, their labels faded beyond recognition. But it was the center of the room that drew their attention – a circular platform covered in symbols similar to those in Marie's book.

"It's a waypoint," Mills realized, his enhanced vision picking out details Marissa couldn't see. "Part of the sigil the Comte's creating across the city."

"Look." Marissa pointed to a fresh carving on one of the support columns. The same symbol that had been carved into Elena's wrist, still wet with what could only be blood.

"He's been here recently." Mills' nostrils flared. "Within the last hour. This is all part of his plan – forcing us down here, marking the old places with his power."

Another scream, much closer now. The temperature in the chamber dropped rapidly, frost crystallizing on the ancient bottles.

"The platform," Marissa urged. "If it's part of his sigil, maybe we can use it."

They stepped onto the circular design just as three white-clad figures appeared in the passage they'd come through. The brides moved with fluid grace, their dead eyes fixed on Marissa with horrible hunger.

The one in front – the same one who had watched Marissa sleep – smiled with bloodstained lips. "Little siren," she sang, her voice carrying echoes of what she'd been before the Comte turned her. "Your power calls to us. Your blood sings such sweet songs."

"Marie's daughter," Mills murmured. "The one she wants us to destroy."

The bride's smile widened. "Mother sent you to kill me? How... predictable." She glided forward, her sisters flanking her in perfect synchronization. "But she doesn't understand. What I've become, what the Comte offers... it's beyond her small ambitions."

"What is he really planning?" Marissa demanded. "What's the ritual really for?"

"Wouldn't you like to know?" The bride's laugh was like breaking glass. "Ask your detective. Ask him what he really saw in Baton Rouge five years ago. Ask him why the Comte chose him specifically for mutation."

Mills tensed beside her. "What are you talking about?"

"Oh, this is delicious. He really doesn't remember." The bride's dead eyes gleamed. "The Comte's power touched you long before now, Detective. Why do you think you've taken to the change so naturally? Why your hunger is so controlled compared to most newborns?"

"Mills?" Marissa looked up at him, seeing confusion and dawning horror in his eyes.

"I don't—" He stopped, fangs extending as ancient memories tried to surface. "The compound in Baton Rouge. There was something... something I saw..."

"Remember," the bride sang, her voice carrying that same supernatural power that had affected Marissa before. "Remember what you really are."

Mills' grip on Marissa's hand became painfully tight as images flooded his mind. She could feel him trembling with the force of recovered memories.

"The vampire I killed," he whispered. "He wasn't trying to fight me. He was trying to warn me. About what I'd been, what I'd forgotten..."

"Very good." The bride took another step forward. "You're one of us, Detective. Have been since that night thirty years ago, when the Comte first tasted your blood. He just... suppressed the changes. Until now."

The revelation hit Marissa like a physical blow. Mills wasn't just temporarily transformed – he was reclaiming a vampire nature he'd carried unknowingly for decades.

"The ritual," she realized. "It's not just about the city. It's about awakening others like him. Sleeper vampires hidden throughout New Orleans."

"Smart little siren." The bride's smile was terrible in its beauty. "Tomorrow night, when the veil is thinnest and the power flows freely... everyone who's ever been touched by the Comte's blood will remember what they truly are. And New Orleans will become what it was always meant to be – a city of the night."

"How many?" Mills demanded, his voice rough with horror. "How many are there like me?"

"Hundreds. Maybe thousands. Policemen, politicians, priests... all carrying dormant vampire blood, just waiting for the Comte's signal to awaken." The bride spread her arms wide. "Can you imagine it? An entire city becoming blood sucking creatures in a single night?"

The symbols beneath their feet began to glow with sickly green light. The bride's eyes widened.

"Ah," she said softly. "Mother's clever wards are activating. But it doesn't matter. We'll see you both tomorrow night, at the ball." Her dead eyes fixed on Marissa. "Save a dance for us, little siren. We so look forward to tasting your power."

The light from the platform grew blinding. Marissa felt Mills pull her close, shielding her with his body as reality seemed to twist and bend around them.

The last thing she heard before the teleportation took hold was the bride's haunting laugh, and her final warning:

"Run all you want, but you can't escape what's coming. The night will claim its own, and blood will remember blood."

Then the world dissolved into emerald fire, and they were falling through spaces that should not exist, toward a destination that could only be determined by the Comte's carefully laid plans.

The game had changed completely. Mills wasn't just playing at being a vampire – he was one of the Comte's lost children, a sleeper agent who had never known his true nature.

And tomorrow night, when the ritual began, every other sleeper in New Orleans would awaken to their vampire heritage.

The city didn't stand a chance.

Unless they could find a way to stop it in the next twenty-four hours.

The real question was: could Mills fight against his own true nature? Or would blood remember blood, as the bride had promised?

They were about to find out.

And the answer would determine the fate of everyone in New Orleans.

Chapter 8: Buried Truths

The teleportation magic dumped them in Lafayette Cemetery, among crumbling tombs and ancient oaks draped with Spanish moss. Mills caught Marissa before she could stumble, his strength and reflexes moving faster than thought. The contact sent electricity through his nervous system, along with a surge of hunger he fought to suppress.

"You need to get away from me," he growled, forcing himself to release her. The revelations in the catacombs had shaken something loose inside him – memories trying to surface, a nature he'd apparently carried unknowingly for thirty years struggling to break free.

"Mills—"

"I said get back!" His voice emerged as a snarl, fangs fully extended. The hunger was worse now, clawing at his insides with renewed intensity. Everything felt sharper, more primal – like his temporary transformation had merely been a preview of his true nature reasserting itself.

"Detective Mills." Sister Angelique emerged from behind a nearby tomb, her white dress somehow pristine despite the cemetery dirt. "Control yourself. What you're feeling now – the hunger, the rage – it's your buried nature fighting to surface. You must master it, or you'll be worse than useless against the Comte."

Mills closed his eyes, trying to focus past the bloodlust. Marissa's scent filled his heightened senses – jasmine and power and everything he wanted to devour. "You knew," he accused Sister Angelique. "You knew what I really was."

"I suspected." She moved closer, unafraid despite his obvious struggle for control. "There were signs – your unusual success rate with supernatural cases, your ability to resist certain forms of vampire influence. But I couldn't be certain until the transformation ritual. True vampires take to the change differently than humans."

A memory surfaced – fragments of that night in Baton Rouge five years ago. The vampire he'd killed hadn't been begging for mercy. He'd been trying to tell Mills something...

"Brother," the creature had gasped around a mouthful of blood. *"You don't remember, but you're one of us. He made you forget, made all of you forget, but when the time comes..."*

"How many?" Mills demanded, opening his eyes to fix Sister Angelique with a predator's stare. "How many others like me are there in the city?"

"According to Marie's records? At least five hundred confirmed cases over the last century. People who encountered the Comte during his previous visits to New

Orleans, who survived having their blood taken but showed no signs of mutating." She produced a weathered leather journal from somewhere in her voluminous skirts. "But those are only the ones we know about."

"And tomorrow night, when he performs his ritual..." Marissa trailed off, the implications too horrible to voice.

"Every dormant vampire in the city will awaken," Sister Angelique confirmed. "Imagine it – hundreds of newly turned vampires, all linked to the Comte's bloodline, all awakening at once. The chaos alone will transform New Orleans forever."

"It's worse than that." The new voice made them all turn. Cassie emerged from the shadows, looking exhausted but determined. "I've been researching the symbol from Elena's wrist. It's not just about awakening dormant vampires – it's about control. Whoever completes the ritual will have power over every vampire created from their bloodline."

"An instant army," Mills realized. "Loyal to him alone."

"And positioned in every level of city government, law enforcement, and infrastructure," Sister Angelique added. "The perfect coup."

Mills' enhanced vision caught movement among the tombs – shapes in white dresses flitting between the stones. "We're not alone."

"The brides are hunting," Sister Angelique confirmed. "But they won't attack yet. The Comte wants to save that pleasure for tomorrow night."

Another memory surfaced, this one older – thirty years ago, during Mardi Gras. He'd been a rookie cop, working crowd control on Bourbon Street. A well-dressed European gentleman had stopped to ask him directions...

"He took my blood," Mills whispered. "Right there on Bourbon Street, in the middle of Carnival. Everyone was too drunk, too caught up in the festivities to notice. And afterward..."

"He made you forget," Sister Angelique finished. "Made you bury your true nature so deep even you didn't know it was there. Until now."

"Why? Why wait thirty years to activate his sleepers?"

"Because he needed the right circumstances," Cassie said. "The right alignment of power. Mardi Gras has always been when the veil between worlds is thinnest in New Orleans, but some years are more powerful than others." She pulled out her grimoire, flipping to a page covered in astronomical calculations. "Tomorrow night – Fat Tuesday – coincides with a total lunar eclipse. The first one to fall on Mardi Gras in over a century."

"The perfect conditions for his ritual," Sister Angelique agreed. "And he's been preparing for decades, seeding the city with his blood, placing his sleeper agents in positions of power. Tomorrow night, when he awakens them all at once..."

A scream cut through the cemetery – not the supernatural keen of the brides, but something terrifyingly human. Mills moved without thinking, vampire speed carrying him toward the sound. He found the source in front of a massive family tomb.

The victim was young, probably a tourist who'd wandered into the cemetery on one of those ghost tours that were so popular in the Quarter. She lay crumpled at the foot of the tomb, blood still flowing from the twin puncture wounds in her neck. Above her, carved fresh into the stone, was the now-familiar symbol from Elena's wrist.

"He's marking the old places," Cassie said, arriving with the others. "Creating anchor points for tomorrow night's ritual."

Mills knelt beside the victim, his enhanced senses picking up the faintest flutter of a heartbeat. "She's still alive."

"Not for long," Sister Angelique said grimly. "The Comte's brides are efficient feeders."

The hunger rose again as Mills caught the scent of fresh blood. Part of him – the part that was apparently his true nature – wanted nothing more than to finish what the brides had started.

A warm hand touched his shoulder. Marissa knelt beside him, either not noticing or not caring how his eyes fixed on her throat. "You're not like them," she said softly. "Whatever the Comte made you, whatever's buried inside you – you're still you."

"Am I?" He could feel his control slipping, the predator inside him rising. "You heard what the bride said. Blood remembers blood. When he activates the ritual..."

"Then we'll deal with it." Her voice held absolute conviction. "But right now, we need to get her help."

As if in response to her words, the victim's eyes fluttered open. But something was wrong – her pupils were blown wide, and when she spoke, her voice held echoes of a more ancient tongue.

"He comes," she whispered in French. "Le roi des vampires, le maître de la nuit. The king of vampires, master of the night. When the moon bleeds and the masks fall..." She convulsed once, violently. "All will remember. All will serve."

Her eyes rolled back, revealing bloodshot sclera. Mills caught her before she could slam her head against the tomb.

"Possession," Sister Angelique spat. "The Comte is using his victims as messengers."

"We need to get her to a hospital," Marissa insisted.

"No hospital can help her now." Sister Angelique's voice was heavy with centuries of similar losses. "The Comte's brides don't leave survivors. This message was meant for us."

As if to prove her point, the victim's body began to change – her skin graying, her flesh seeming to cave in on itself. Within seconds, she looked as if she'd been dead for days rather than minutes.

"Time magic," Cassie breathed. "He's accelerating her decay."

Mills closed the victim's eyes, his enhanced vision catching something carved into her flesh beneath her collar. Not the Comte's usual symbol, but a series of numbers.

"Coordinates," he realized. "He's giving us an address."

"It's a trap," Sister Angelique said immediately.

"Obviously. But do we have a choice?" Mills stood, fighting back the last remnants of hunger. "He's always been one step ahead of us. Everything that's happened –

Elena's death, my transformation, the brides hunting Marissa – it's all been part of his plan."

"So we spring the trap," Marissa said. "But on our terms."

"No." Mills' voice was firm. "You're not going anywhere near—"

"I'm already involved," she cut him off. "The Comte made sure of that. And like it or not, you need me. We all do."

She was right, and Mills hated it. The protective instinct warring with his hunger was complicated by another feeling he didn't want to examine too closely – something deeper than mere attraction, more primal than simple affection.

"Fine," he growled. "But we do this smart. No splitting up, no heroics." He looked at Sister Angelique. "How long until sunrise?"

"Three hours. Not enough time to prepare properly."

"Then we prepare improperly." Mills could feel his true nature stirring beneath the surface, bringing with it skills and instincts he didn't remember learning. "The Comte wants to play games? Fine. Let's show him we can play too."

A cold wind swept through the cemetery, carrying with it the distant sound of the brides' hunting song. Among the tombs, white dresses flickered like ghost lights, moving steadily closer.

They had three hours until dawn, less than twenty-four until the Comte's ritual began. Somewhere in the city, five hundred dormant vampires waited to be awakened, their buried natures ready to transform New Orleans into a kingdom of eternal night.

And Mills, the detective who'd spent his career fighting supernatural evil, was apparently one of them.

The game was reaching its climax, but the rules had changed completely. The only question was: when blood called to blood and ancient natures awoke, whose side would he really be on?

The brides' song grew louder, and somewhere in his stolen mansion, the Comte raised one final glass of blood in toast to his unwitting pawns.

The true dance was about to begin.

And not everyone would survive to see the morning.

Chapter 9: The Devil's Dance

The coordinates led them to St. Roch Chapel, its weathered facade looming against the pre-dawn sky. Mills could smell old blood and newer death before they even entered – the Comte's brides had been busy tonight.

"Wait." Cassie grabbed his arm as he reached for the door. "There are wards. Strong ones."

Mills' enhanced vision picked out the symbols carved into the door frame – ancient sigils that seemed to writhe and pulse with contained power. "Can you break them?"

"Breaking them isn't the problem." Cassie's fingers traced the air just above the markings. "They're meant to be broken. See how the power flows? When these wards shatter, they'll release something."

"A trap within a trap," Sister Angelique murmured. Her honey-colored eyes seemed to glow in the darkness. "Clever beast."

Marissa stepped closer to examine the wards, and Mills had to fight back a surge of protective instinct mixed with predatory hunger. Her proximity made his borrowed – no, his true – vampire nature stir uncomfortably.

"These symbols," she said, pointing to a particular set of markings. "They're different from the others. Almost like..."

"Like they're waiting for something specific," Cassie finished. She flipped through her grimoire, comparing the symbols to various entries. "Blood magic, but not just any blood. They need..."

"Mine." Mills didn't know how he knew, but the certainty settled into his bones like old cemetery dirt. "The blood of one of his children."

Sister Angelique nodded grimly. "The Comte is forcing you to acknowledge your true nature. To actively participate in his ritual rather than simply being awakened by it."

The implications hung heavy in the pre-dawn air. Mills could feel something stirring in his blood – memories trying to surface, a nature he'd buried so deep even he didn't know it existed. Until now.

"Do it," Marissa said softly. When he turned to look at her, she met his gaze steadily despite his obvious struggle with the hunger. "We need to know what's inside."

Mills drew the silver knife Marie had given him – spelled to cut vampire flesh without healing instantly. The blade bit into his palm, drawing blood darker than human normal. As the first drops hit the wards, the symbols flared with sickly green light.

The door swung open on silent hinges, revealing the chapel's interior. The pews had been pushed to the walls, creating a clear space in the center of the nave. And there, arranged in a perfect circle, were six bodies.

"Jesus Christ," Cassie breathed. Her witch sight must have shown her something even Mills' vampire vision couldn't perceive, because she took an involuntary step back. "The power here..."

Mills moved forward carefully, examining the victims. Each had been posed with elaborate care – hands crossed over their chests, eyes closed as if in sleep. All bore the twin puncture marks of vampire feeding, but these wounds were different. Surgical. Precise.

"They're not dead," he realized, his enhanced hearing picking up the faintest of heartbeats. "Not completely."

"No," Sister Angelique agreed. "They're in transition. Becoming like the brides – but something more. Something worse."

As if summoned by her words, the victims' eyes snapped open in perfect unison. But where the brides' eyes held only death, these burned with an inner fire that spoke of ancient power and older hunger.

They spoke as one, their voices carrying echoes of the Comte's aristocratic French: "Welcome, my children. To the final rehearsal."

Mills moved instantly, placing himself between the possessed victims and Marissa. But the bodies made no move to attack. They simply sat up, movements puppet-like and wrong, smiles identical and terrible.

"Did you think I wouldn't plan for this?" the Comte spoke through his puppets. "That I wouldn't account for every variable, every possible interference?" The victims' heads tilted at identical angles. "Detective Mills. My prodigal son. How does it feel to remember what you truly are?"

"I'm nothing like you," Mills growled, though the hunger rising in his blood suggested otherwise.

"No? Then why can you smell the power in the little siren's blood? Why do you dream of tasting it, of making her one of us?" The Comte's laugh emerged from six throats simultaneously. "Blood remembers blood, Detective. And tomorrow night, when the moon bleeds and the masks fall... all my children will remember their true nature."

Marissa stepped forward, either ignoring or not noticing how Mills tensed at her movement. "Why show us this? Why lead us here?"

"Because, my dear, every performance needs a proper audience. And you..." The possessed victims' smiles widened impossibly. "You have a particularly important role to play."

Before anyone could react, the victims began to change. Their flesh seemed to ripple and flow like wax, revealing something ancient and horrible beneath the human disguise. The transformation happened too quickly for even Mills' enhanced vision to track.

Where six human bodies had been, six creatures now crouched – things that looked like crosses between vampires and something much, much older. Their skin was pale as moonlight but seemed to shift and writhe with patterns just below the surface. Their eyes burned with the same fire as before, but now that fire seemed to consume their entire being.

"Beautiful, aren't they?" the Comte's voice emerged from their twisted mouths. "The next stage of vampire evolution. Tomorrow night, when the ritual is complete, all my children will have the opportunity to ascend to this new form. To become something greater than mere immortals."

"They're abominations," Sister Angelique spat. "You're violating the natural order itself."

"The natural order?" The creatures laughed with their maker's voice. "I am older than your concepts of nature, little priestess. I have seen empires rise and fall, watched humanity crawl from the mud of creation. And now, at last, the stars are aligned for my greatest work."

The creatures rose with liquid grace, moving in perfect synchronization. Mills could smell the power rolling off them in waves – something ancient and wrong, like time itself had begun to rot.

"Consider this a preview," the Comte said through his creations. "A taste of what's to come. Tomorrow night, when my children awaken and ascend... New Orleans will become the birthplace of a new species."

The creatures launched themselves forward with impossible speed. Even Mills' vampire reflexes barely registered their movement before they were upon them.

The battle that followed was chaos. Cassie's magic flared bright and deadly, but the creatures seemed to absorb her spells like water. Sister Angelique's powers fared better, her frost magic actually managing to slow them down.

But it was Mills who truly understood the horror of what they faced. Because part of him – the buried vampire nature now struggling to surface – recognized these things. Knew them on a cellular level.

This was what the Comte's blood was capable of. What all his children could become.

What he could become.

The thought distracted him just long enough for one of the creatures to slip past his guard. It moved with liquid speed toward Marissa, claws extended...

Mills didn't think. He moved on pure instinct, vampire strength and speed pushing his transformed body to its limits. He caught the creature in mid-leap, feeling its flesh writhe and shift under his grip like something trying to exist in too many dimensions at once.

"Excellent!" the Comte's voice emerged from the creature's twisted mouth. "You see? The power is there, waiting to be claimed. Embrace it, my son. Become what you were always meant to be."

Instead, Mills drove his silver knife into the creature's chest. It screamed with six voices at once, its flesh beginning to dissolve like wax under a flame.

The other creatures paused in their attack, heads tilting at identical angles. "As you wish," they said in the Comte's voice. "But remember – when the blood calls tomorrow night, you won't be able to resist its song. None of my children will."

They moved as one, flowing like liquid shadow toward the chapel doors. In seconds, they were gone, leaving behind only the scent of ancient power and rotting time.

"Well," Cassie said into the heavy silence that followed. "That was..."

"A warning," Sister Angelique finished. "And a promise." She turned to Mills, her honey-colored eyes grave. "You felt it, didn't you? The pull of his blood, the offer of transformation?"

Mills nodded stiffly, still fighting the hunger that the combat had awakened. "If that's what he can do to ordinary humans... what happens tomorrow night when he awakens five hundred vampires at once?"

"Chaos," Marissa said softly. "Complete chaos. Unless..."

"Unless what?"

She met his eyes steadily, despite the predatory light he knew burned in them. "Unless we can find a way to break his hold on his bloodline. To free you – all of you – from his influence before the ritual begins."

"That's impossible," Sister Angelique started to say, but Cassie cut her off.

"Maybe not." The witch was already flipping through her grimoire. "There's an old ritual – dangerous, probably suicidal, but... it might work. If we had the right ingredients. And the right bait."

Mills didn't like where this was going. "What kind of bait?"

"Someone with power in their blood," Cassie said carefully, not looking at Marissa. "Someone who could draw the Comte's attention at a crucial moment. Long enough for the ritual to take effect."

"Absolutely not," Mills growled, moving closer to Marissa without conscious thought. "We're not using her as bait."

"We might not have a choice," Marissa pointed out. "The Comte's already marked me. He's been watching me, planning this whole thing from the start. Maybe... maybe we can use that against him."

Before Mills could protest further, a new sound cut through the pre-dawn air – bells tolling from St. Louis Cathedral, marking the hour before sunrise.

"Dawn's coming," Sister Angelique said. "We need to move. The Comte's creatures may be gone, but the brides are still hunting."

They left the chapel quickly, Mills fighting his vampire nature's aversion to the approaching sun. But as they emerged into the gradually lightening sky, a final message echoed in his mind – the Comte's voice, carried on bonds of blood and ancient power:

"The stage is set, my children. Tomorrow night, we dance the devil's dance. And New Orleans will never be the same."

The sun rose over the French Quarter, painting the sky in colors that reminded Mills too much of blood. In less than eighteen hours, the Comte would begin his ritual.

And Mills would either find a way to break free of his maker's blood...

Or become something that would make the brides look tame by comparison.

The clock was ticking.

And in his mansion on Burgundy Street, the Comte raised a final glass of blood, toasting the chaos to come.

The real horror was about to begin.

Chapter 10: Shadows of Yesterday

Dawn found them in Sister Angelique's sanctuary, a former convent converted into a fortress against supernatural threats. Mills paced the darkened basement like a caged predator, fighting both the sun's pull toward vampire sleep and the memories trying to surface from thirty years of enforced forgetting.

"Drink this." Sister Angelique handed him a crystal goblet filled with something too dark to be wine. "It will help with the daylight sensitivity, though you won't enjoy the taste."

She wasn't wrong. The liquid burned worse than silver, carrying hints of graveyard dirt and older, stranger elements. But it did seem to dull the sun's call, allowing him to focus on the more pressing problem of his fragmenting memories.

"Tell me what you remember," Marissa said softly from her position by one of the basement's heavily warded windows. She looked exhausted but determined, the protection charms at her throat pulsing with steady power. "About that night thirty years ago."

Mills closed his eyes, letting the buried memories surface. "I was working Carnival crowd control on Bourbon Street. Rookie beat cop, first major holiday assignment. The Comte... he seemed so normal at first. Well-dressed tourist asking for directions to Jackson Square."

The memory crystallized with vampire clarity: *The European gentleman's perfect manners, his aristocratic French accent. The way the crowd seemed to flow around them like water, no one noticing as he stepped too close...*

"He thanked me for my assistance," Mills continued, his hand going unconsciously to his throat. "Said he had a gift for the helpful young officer. I remember his eyes – ancient, hungry. Then pain, but... pleasant pain. Like falling into warm water."

"The vampire's kiss," Sister Angelique explained. "Their bite carries a supernatural narcotic effect. Makes the victims compliant, eager even."

"After that, it's fragments. He made me drink something... his blood, I realize now. Said I was to be part of something greater, that when the time was right..." Mills stopped, fangs extending as another memory hit: *The taste of immortal blood, power beyond imagining flowing into him, changing him on a cellular level...*

"He was creating sleeper agents," Cassie said from where she sat surrounded by ancient texts. "Hiding his children in plain sight until he needed them."

"But why make them forget?" Marissa asked. "Why not just turn them fully?"

"Because fully turned vampires are obvious," Sister Angelique answered. "They can't walk in daylight, can't eat normal food, can't hide what they are. But partial transformations, sealed away behind mental blocks..." She gestured to Mills. "They can live entire human lives, never knowing what they truly are. Until their maker calls them to wake."

The basement door opened, admitting McBride. The detective looked like he hadn't slept in days, his clothes rumpled and stained with what might have been blood.

"You need to see this," he said without preamble, dropping a file on the table. "Started digging into unsolved cases from the Comte's previous visits to New Orleans. Found something interesting about the 1837 yellow fever epidemic."

Mills moved to examine the file, his enhanced vision easily reading the faded text. "Mass graves," he said after a moment. "Hundreds of bodies buried in unmarked plots throughout the city."

"Not just hundreds," McBride corrected. "Thousands. And get this – when they exhumed some of them during a construction project in the 1950s, they found something weird. Every single body had the same mark carved into their wrist."

He produced a photograph that made Mills' borrowed – no, his true – vampire blood run cold. The symbol was instantly recognizable: the same one carved into Elena's flesh, the same one appearing at each of the Comte's ritual sites.

"It wasn't just a yellow fever epidemic," Sister Angelique said grimly. "It was a mass turning. The Comte tried to create his vampire army then, but something went wrong. The turnings failed, leaving only corpses behind."

"Because the alignment wasn't right," Cassie added, consulting her grimoire. "Tonight's conditions – Mardi Gras coinciding with a total lunar eclipse – they only happen once every century or so. He's been planning this for a very, very long time."

"There's more." McBride pulled out another file. "Started running background checks on prominent city figures. People in positions of power – judges, police captains, city council members. Found something interesting about their family histories."

Mills already knew what the file would show, but seeing it laid out in black and white made it horrifyingly real. Every person on McBride's list had an ancestor who'd encountered the Comte during one of his previous visits to New Orleans.

"Blood remembers blood," he quoted softly. "He didn't just create sleeper agents thirty years ago. He's been seeding his bloodline through the city's power structure for centuries."

"Building toward this moment," Sister Angelique agreed. "When the stars align perfectly and the veil is thinnest, he'll awaken not just your generation of sleepers, but every dormant vampire blood connection he's created over the centuries."

The implications were staggering. Hundreds, maybe thousands of people carrying dormant vampire genes, all awakening at once to their true nature. And all of them bound by blood to serve the Comte's will.

"We're missing something," Marissa said suddenly. She moved to examine the files, her fingers tracing the familiar symbol. "This isn't just about creating an army. The ritual sites, the specific victims, the timing... it's all too precise."

"She's right." Cassie joined her, comparing the symbol to various entries in her grimoire. "This pattern... it's not just a sigil for awakening dormant vampires. It's something older. Something worse."

Before she could elaborate, a sound cut through the basement's heavy silence – singing, beautiful and terrible, coming from everywhere and nowhere at once.

The brides' hunting song.

But this was different from their previous attacks. The music carried power that made Mills' vampire nature stir uncomfortably, calling to something buried deep in his transformed blood.

"They're not hunting," he realized, feeling the pull of the song in his bones. "They're calling. Trying to wake the sleepers early."

Around the city, he knew, others like him would be feeling this call. Fighting against thirty years of enforced forgetting as their true nature tried to surface ahead of schedule.

"Mills." Marissa's voice cut through the song's power. She stood before him, either not noticing or not caring how his eyes had gone fully vampire in response to the brides' call. "Stay with us. Focus on my voice."

He tried, but the song was inside him now, awakening memories he'd rather stayed buried. The night the Comte took his blood. The power that had flowed into him. The promise of transformation into something greater than human...

"Detective Mills." Sister Angelique's voice cracked like a whip. "Control yourself. Remember what you are."

"That's the problem," he growled, feeling his fangs extend fully. "I'm remembering exactly what I am."

The song grew stronger, and with it came images – the Comte's private chambers, seen through the eyes of his brides. The ritual preparations. The ancient power gathering for tonight's transformation.

And something else... something the brides weren't meant to show him.

"The book," he gasped, fighting against the song's pull. "In his study. I saw..."

"What?" Marissa stepped closer, her warm hand cupping his cold cheek. The contact helped ground him against the supernatural compulsion. "What did you see?"

"The true ritual. Not just transformation, but... ascension. He's not trying to create an army." Mills met her eyes, hoping she could see the horror of what he'd glimpsed. "He's trying to create a new species. Using his bloodline as a foundation to remake humanity itself."

The song cut off abruptly, leaving behind a silence that rang with implications. In the distance, church bells began to toll noon.

They had eight hours until sunset.

Eight hours to find a way to stop a ritual that had been centuries in the making.

Eight hours before Mills and every other sleeper vampire in New Orleans would be called to embrace their true nature.

And somewhere in his mansion on Burgundy Street, the Comte raised yet another glass of blood, toasting the audience he knew was watching through his brides' eyes.

The final act was approaching.

And not even Sister Angelique's wards could protect them from what was coming.

Because the enemy wasn't just the Comte anymore.

The enemy was the blood in Mills' own veins.

And it was getting harder and harder to resist its call.

Chapter 11: Blood Awakening

The first attack came at two in the afternoon.

Detective Megan Marshall, fifteen-year veteran of the NOPD, was in the middle of questioning a shoplifting suspect when the headache hit. By the time backup arrived, they found her crouched over the suspect's body, fangs extended, ancient blood awakening decades before schedule.

The second incident occurred thirty minutes later at City Hall. Judge Michael Broussard, halfway through sentencing a drug dealer, suddenly stopped mid-word. When the bailiff approached to check on him, the judge's eyes had gone completely black.

They lost contact with three precincts in the next hour.

Mills watched the reports flood in on McBride's laptop, each new incident confirming his worst fears. The Comte's influence was spreading faster than they'd anticipated, the dormant vampire blood in his sleeper agents responding to some signal they couldn't yet detect.

"It's starting early," Sister Angelique said grimly. "The lunar eclipse is pulling at the blood bonds, weakening the seals he placed on his children."

"We're running out of time." Cassie hadn't slept in over twenty-four hours, her fingers stained with herbs and darker substances as she worked on protection charms. "If they're turning now, before the ritual..."

"Then by midnight, the entire city could be overrun," Mills finished. His own blood was burning, memories continuing to surface with vampire clarity. Every mutated sleeper agent added to the pressure building in his veins, calling him to embrace his true nature.

Marissa appeared at his side, offering a thermos that smelled of Sister Angelique's spelled blood substitute. Her proximity made his fangs ache, but the hunger was becoming easier to control. Or maybe he was just getting better at hiding it.

"There's something we're not seeing," she said, spreading out the case files they'd accumulated. "The Comte's previous attempts, the failed mass turning in 1837... what changed? Why is it working now?"

Mills forced himself to focus on the documents rather than the pulse in her throat. "The alignment is different. Mardi Gras coinciding with the eclipse..."

"No." Cassie looked up from her grimoire suddenly. "That's not the only thing that's changed. Look at the victims he's chosen this time. Elena, Catherine, Marie... they all had something in common besides being young and beautiful."

"Power," Sister Angelique realized. "Each one had some form of supernatural potential. Elena was a latent medium, Catherine came from a family of weather workers..."

"He's not just creating vampires," Mills said as the pieces clicked together. "He's creating conduits. Each death adds their power to his ritual, creating..." He stopped as a new memory surfaced, this one from the night the Comte had taken his blood.

"You'll be more than merely immortal, my son. When the time comes, you'll help birth a new species. Something that combines vampire strength with human magic, that can walk in daylight and command the very forces of nature..."

"An evolutionary leap," Marissa whispered. "He's trying to create supernatural hybrids. Vampires who can use magic, who aren't bound by traditional limitations."

"And he's using his sleeper agents as the foundation," Cassie added. "People who've carried vampire blood for years, whose bodies have adapted to the change on a cellular level."

Before anyone could respond, Mills' phone rang. The caller ID showed McBride.

"We've got another problem," his partner said without preamble. "Just got a call from Marie Delacroix. The Black Rose has been attacked."

Mills felt his borrowed – no, his true – vampire strength surge with alarm. "The brides?"

"Worse. Some of the newly awakened sleepers broke in searching for blood. Marie's security handled most of them, but... they got into her private vault. Stole something she says changes everything."

"What did they take?"

Marie's voice came on the line, her usual aristocratic calm shattered. "The Grimoire of Saint-Germain. My brother recovered it from the Comte's original lab in Paris, centuries ago. It contains the full ritual he's planning for tonight. And a list of every sleeper agent he's created in the past three hundred years."

The implications hit Mills like a physical blow. "He knows who all of his children are. Every single one."

"Yes," Marie hissed. "And with that book, he can wake them all at once. No waiting for the eclipse, no complex ritual needed. Just pure blood magic, powered by centuries of careful breeding and selection."

As if to emphasize her words, a new wave of pressure built in Mills' transformed blood. Memories flooded his consciousness – not just from thirty years ago, but older. Much older.

"Mills?" Marissa's voice seemed to come from far away. "What's wrong?"

"It's not just my blood," he managed through extended fangs. "It's... generations. My grandfather disappeared during the Comte's 1937 visit. And his grandmother before that, during the yellow fever epidemic..."

"Blood remembers blood," Sister Angelique quoted grimly. "He didn't just create sleeper agents. He created entire bloodlines of them, passing the dormant vampire traits down through generations."

"And now he can activate them all," Cassie whispered. "Every person in New Orleans who carries even a trace of his blood in their family tree..."

Mills' hearing picked up new sirens in the distance. More attacks, more sleeper agents awakening ahead of schedule. The pressure in his blood was becoming unbearable, ancient power calling to power.

"We need to move," he demanded. "Now. Before—"

The world exploded in supernatural agony. Mills felt his knees hit the floor as every drop of the Comte's blood in his veins seemed to ignite at once. Through the pain, he heard Marissa calling his name, felt her warm hands on his cold skin.

But stronger than that was a new voice – ancient, powerful, speaking directly to the vampire nature he'd carried unknowingly for three decades:

"Rise, my children. The time of hiding is over. Embrace what you truly are..."

The Comte's command reverberated through blood and bone, calling to something deeper than mere genetics. Mills fought against it, focusing on Marissa's touch, on the mission, on anything but the supernatural compulsion trying to remake him from the inside out.

But across the city, others were listening. Others were answering. Others were embracing their true nature with terrible enthusiasm.

The metamorphosis had begun.

And they had less than six hours to stop it before New Orleans became ground zero for the evolution of an entirely new species.

The clock was ticking.

And somewhere in his mansion on Burgundy Street, surrounded by newly awakened children of his blood, the

Comte began the final preparations for a ritual three centuries in the making.

    The real horror was about to begin.

    And not even Sister Angelique's strongest wards could protect them from what was coming.

    Because the enemy wasn't just out there anymore.

    The enemy was in Mills' own veins.

    And it was winning.

Chapter 12: The Hour of the Wolf

The city was burning.

From Sister Angelique's sanctuary, Mills watched New Orleans descend into chaos as more sleeper agents awakened. Police scanners crackled with reports of attacks across all districts – seemingly normal citizens suddenly transforming, their dormant vampire blood responding to the Comte's call.

"Eighth precinct is gone," McBride reported grimly through Mills' phone. "Captain Thibodeaux turned first, then half the force followed. They've barricaded themselves inside, and..." He paused, the sound of distant screaming coming through the line. "Jesus Christ. The ones they've caught, they're not just feeding. They're... changing them. Making more."

"It's exponential growth," Sister Angelique said, her honey-colored eyes fixed on the map they'd spread across her work table. Red pins marked confirmed transformations, black pins for sites of massive turnings.

The pattern was horrifyingly clear – the Comte's influence spreading outward from the French Quarter like a bloodstain. "Each newly awakened vampire is creating more, building his army faster than we can track."

Mills fought another wave of pressure in his transformed blood. The Comte's call was stronger now, a constant pull toward embracing his true nature. Only Marissa's presence kept him grounded, though being near her brought its own kind of torment.

"The hospitals are being overwhelmed," Cassie reported, scrolling through emergency alerts on her laptop. "They're trying to pass it off as some kind of mass hysteria, but..." She turned the screen to show surveillance footage from Tulane Medical Center. The images showed doctors and nurses with extended fangs, turning their own patients into food and fodder for the Comte's growing forces.

"We need to move against him now," Mills growled. "Before his army gets any larger."

"Agreed," Marie Delacroix's voice came through the speaker phone. "But we have a more immediate problem. My sources say he's sending his newly awakened children to specific locations throughout the city. Places of power – churches, cemeteries, crossroads. They're preparing the ground for something."

"The ritual sites," Marissa realized, examining the map. "Look at the pattern – each major incident forms another point in his sigil. He's using the chaos to complete the symbol he started with the original murders."

Mills studied the map with vampire vision, seeing what human eyes couldn't – lines of power connecting each site, forming a massive occult circuit with the

Comte's mansion at its center. "It's not just a symbol anymore. It's a machine. A supernatural engine powered by blood and transformation."

"Designed to do what?" McBride demanded.

"To break down the barriers between species," Sister Angelique said grimly. "To use the combined power of all his awakened children to fuel an evolution jump. To create something entirely new."

Before anyone could respond, the pressure in Mills' blood spiked again. This time the pain dropped him to his knees, ancient memories surfacing with vampire clarity.

Not just thirty years ago on Bourbon Street. Earlier. Much earlier. His grandfather disappearing during the Comte's 1937 visit, but not before passing on the changed blood to his son. And before that, his great-grandmother during the yellow fever epidemic, surviving just long enough to bear a child carrying vampire genetics...

"Mills?" Marissa's warm hand on his cold cheek helped him focus through the supernatural agony. "Stay with us."

"The bloodlines," he gasped. "It's not random. He chose us carefully, bred us across generations to carry specific traits. Powers that would activate when the change came..."

As if to prove his point, the pain suddenly translated into something else – power flooding his transformed nervous system. His vampire sight expanded exponentially, letting him see through walls, through flesh, through time itself...

"My God," Sister Angelique breathed. "You're manifesting abilities. The hybrid powers the Comte designed his bloodline to carry."

Mills could see them now – threads of possibility and power connecting everyone in the room. Could see the latent magic in Marissa's blood calling to his own transformed nature. Could see the carefully crafted genetic patterns the Comte had woven through generations of his chosen bloodlines.

"It's happening across the city," Marie reported, real fear in her ancient voice. "The newly awakened aren't just turning into ordinary vampires. They're developing powers – psychic abilities, control over natural forces, things vampires shouldn't be capable of."

"Because they're not just vampires anymore," Cassie said, consulting her grimoire. "They're something new. Hybrids of vampire strength and human magic, exactly like the Comte planned."

Mills forced himself back to his feet, fighting to control his expanded senses. "How long until sunset?"

"Three hours," Sister Angelique answered. "But I don't think we can wait that long. The Comte has the grimoire now – he can complete his ritual ahead of schedule if he has enough power gathered."

"Then we move now," Mills decided. "Hit his mansion before he can—"

A new sound cut through the chaos of the city – bells tolling from St. Louis Cathedral, but wrong somehow. The notes carried supernatural power that made Mills' enhanced senses scream in warning.

"That's not the regular bell-ringer," Marissa said, moving to the window. "Look."

They watched in horror as white-clad figures scaled the cathedral's tower like spiders, their movements impossibly graceful. The brides had taken the cathedral, and now they were using its bells to broadcast something worse than their hunting song.

The sound transformed into pure power, resonating with the Comte's blood in Mills' veins. Across the city, he knew, every sleeper agent who hadn't yet awakened would be feeling this call.

"No," he growled, fighting against the compulsion. "I won't—"

But his body was already changing, the temporary transformation becoming something deeper, more permanent. He could feel his true nature surfacing, three generations of carefully bred vampire genetics responding to their maker's call.

"Mills." Marissa stepped closer despite Sister Angelique's warning gesture. "Look at me. Focus on my voice."

He tried, but the power flooding his system was overwhelming. His enhanced vision showed him too much – the pulse of magic in her blood, the potential for transformation, the carefully woven patterns of fate that had brought them to this moment...

"The ritual," he gasped through extended fangs. "It's not just about creating hybrids. It's about... choosing. Selecting which bloodlines are worthy of ascension."

"What do you mean?" Sister Angelique demanded.

"The Comte... he's been breeding us like cattle. Creating specific combinations of vampire blood and human magic, testing different mixtures across generations. And now..." Mills looked at Marissa with horror. "Now he's activating the ones that worked. Culling the failed experiments."

As if to prove his point, new screams erupted across the city – different from the earlier chaos. These were sounds of agony as sleeper agents whose bloodlines didn't meet the Comte's standards began to self-destruct.

"My God," McBride's voice came through the phone. "They're... melting. The ones that aren't transforming properly, they're just... Jesus Christ."

Mills could see it through his enhanced vision – people dissolving into masses of twisted flesh and failed transformation, their bodies rejecting the vampire blood that had lurked in their genetics for generations.

But others... others were becoming something magnificent and terrible. Perfect hybrids of vampire power and human magic, exactly as the Comte had planned.

"The final selection," Sister Angelique whispered. "He's choosing his new species. Right now. Using the whole city as his laboratory."

The bells tolled again, and this time Mills couldn't fight the change. His body began to transform at a cellular level, generations of careful breeding coming to fruition.

The last thing he saw clearly was Marissa's face as she caught him, her warm hands cradling his cold flesh as his true nature finally, fully awakened.

Then the world dissolved into blood and power and the sound of ancient bells calling a new species into existence.

The hour of transformation had begun.

And somewhere in his mansion on Burgundy Street, surrounded by his successfully awakened children, the Comte prepared to welcome the newest members of his carefully crafted bloodline.

The real question wasn't whether they could stop him anymore.

The question was: what would be left of New Orleans when his great work was complete?

And more importantly: what would be left of Mills himself?

Chapter 13: The Darkest Hour

The awakening was excruciating and beautiful.

Mills felt every cell in his body realigning, three generations of carefully bred vampire genetics finally expressing their true nature. His consciousness expanded beyond normal limits, letting him perceive layers of reality his human mind had never been equipped to process.

He could see the threads of fate binding everyone in Sister Angelique's sanctuary. Could see the carefully woven patterns of bloodlines and power the Comte had crafted across centuries. Could see the true nature of Marissa's latent abilities calling to his transformed blood...

"Fight it," Marissa's voice cut through the hurricane of new sensations. She held him as his body reshaped itself, either not noticing or not caring how his fangs had extended fully. "Stay with us, Mills."

"The bloodlines," he gasped, ancient memories surfacing with perfect clarity. "I can see them all now. Every choice, every breeding pair, every calculated marriage arranged to produce specific combinations of vampire blood and human magic..."

"Focus," Sister Angelique commanded. Her honey-colored eyes blazed with power as she worked complex spells meant to slow his transformation. "What else can you see?"

Mills' vision pierced through walls and distance, showing him the chaos engulfing New Orleans. Successful hybrids were emerging across the city – former sleeper agents whose bloodlines met the Comte's exacting standards. But others...

"They're dying," he whispered, watching people dissolve into twisted masses of failed transformation. "The ones whose blood isn't pure enough, whose genetics don't match his plans... they're being culled."

"How many?" Marie's voice came through the speaker phone, ancient and afraid. "How many are surviving the change?"

"Maybe one in ten." Mills forced himself to watch through his new senses as the Comte's great work reshaped the city's population. "The ones who make it... they're powerful. More than vampire, more than human. Exactly what he designed us to be."

As if to prove his point, new abilities continued to manifest in his transformed body. Telepathy sharp enough to catch fragments of thoughts from everyone in the room. Telekinesis that made objects shift without conscious effort. And something deeper, more primal – the power to manipulate reality itself at a molecular level.

"The hybrid powers are stabilizing," Sister Angelique observed, her witch sight tracking the changes in his aura.

"The Comte designed each bloodline to carry specific abilities. Yours seems particularly... comprehensive."

"Because he's been breeding my family longer than most," Mills realized, another generation of memories surfacing. "My great-grandmother during the yellow fever epidemic, carrying the first iteration of his blood. Then my grandfather in 1937, receiving an upgraded strain. My own transformation thirty years ago, adding the final elements..."

"A masterwork bloodline," Marie said grimly. "One of his most carefully crafted breeding programs, designed to produce exactly the kind of hybrid he wanted."

Before Mills could respond, the cathedral bells tolled again – not the regular bells, but the twisted versions the brides were using to broadcast the Comte's power. The sound carried supernatural harmonics that made Mills' enhanced senses scream with recognition.

Through his expanded perception, he could see the effect rippling across New Orleans. More sleeper agents awakening, their dormant vampire blood responding to frequencies that had been encoded in their genetics generations ago. More transformations beginning. More culling of bloodlines deemed impure.

"The pattern," Marissa said suddenly, studying the map with new understanding. "The transformation sites aren't random. They're forming..."

"A neural network," Mills finished, his hybrid vision showing him the true design. "The successful transformations are creating a living circuit across the city. Each new hybrid becoming a node in a vast supernatural machine, all connected through the Comte's blood."

"Connected to what purpose?" Sister Angelique demanded.

Before Mills could answer, his phone rang. McBride's voice came through thick with horror: "You need to see this. The ones who survived, they're... building something."

The detective sent a video that made Mills' new hybrid senses recoil. Across New Orleans, the successfully mutated were gathering materials – both mundane and mystical. Working with masterful precision to construct devices that seemed to exist in multiple dimensions at once.

"Focus your vision," Marie instructed. "Look beyond the physical components. What are they really building?"

Mills let his perception expand further, seeing through the veils of reality to the true nature of the constructions. "They're... amplifiers. Designed to channel and focus supernatural energy. But not just any energy..."

"The power of transition itself," Sister Angelique whispered. "He's building a machine to harvest the energy released by mass transfiguration, using it to fuel something even larger."

As if responding to her words, the cathedral bells tolled again. This time the sound carried more than just awakening frequencies – it carried instructions, knowledge encoded in supernatural harmonics that only hybrid senses could properly perceive.

"No," Mills growled, fighting against the compulsion buried in the sound. "He's trying to..."

But his body was already moving, hybrid instincts responding to programs written into his blood generations ago. His hands began sketching designs in the air, reality warping around his fingers as he unconsciously contributed to the Comte's great work.

"Mills!" Marissa grabbed his hands, her touch burning against his cold skin. "What are you doing?"

"The knowledge is in our blood," he managed through extended fangs. "Everything we need to know to build his machine, to complete his transformation engine... he encoded it into our genetics, designed us to be both the power source and the builders..."

"The entire city is becoming a vast supernatural battery," Sister Angelique realized. "Every successful transformation adding more energy, every hybrid adding their unique abilities to the construction..."

"But what is he powering?" McBride demanded through the phone. "What could possibly need that much supernatural energy?"

The answer came to Mills in a flash of hybrid insight, centuries of careful breeding and planning becoming suddenly, horrifyingly clear. "Not what. Who."

"Explain," Marie commanded.

"The Comte... he's not just creating a new species. He's preparing a vessel. A perfect hybrid form capable of containing power beyond anything natural reality can support." Mills looked at them with eyes that now saw far too much. "He's building himself a god body. And we're all just batteries to power his ascension."

The implications hung in the air like cemetery mist. Across New Orleans, thousands of carefully bred bloodlines were activating, their transformations feeding power into a machine designed to elevate its creator beyond mere immortality.

And Mills, carrying one of the Comte's masterwork bloodlines, was being compelled to help build the very engine of apotheosis.

"How long?" Marissa asked, still holding his hands, still anchoring him against the tide of hybrid instincts.

"Hours. Maybe less." He could feel the changes accelerating across the city, feel the power building in the supernatural circuit being constructed by thousands of hybrid hands. "Once enough of us transform, once the network is complete..."

"Then we have to move now," Sister Angelique said. "Before—"

The cathedral bells tolled one final time, and reality itself seemed to shudder. Mills' hybrid senses showed him the truth – the Comte, surrounded by his most successful children, beginning the final phase of a plan three centuries in the making.

The transformation of New Orleans was nearly complete.

The birth of a dark god was about to begin.

And somewhere in Mills' hybrid blood, encoded in genetics crafted across generations, was the key to either stopping it...

Or ensuring its terrible success.

The question was: could he fight against his own carefully designed nature long enough to make the choice?

They were about to find out.

And the fate of not just New Orleans, but reality itself, hung in the balance.

Chapter 14: Echoes of Divinity

The construction of a god required precision.

Through his newly awakened hybrid senses, Mills watched the Comte's great work unfold across New Orleans. Successful perversion continued throughout the city, each new hybrid adding their unique abilities to the vast supernatural machine being built through instincts encoded in their very blood.

The cathedral bells had fallen silent, but their message remained – knowledge buried in supernatural harmonics, compelling every surviving member of the Comte's carefully bred bloodlines to contribute to his ascension. Mills could feel the pull in his own hybrid genetics, generations of careful breeding demanding he take his place in the grand design.

"The network is stabilizing," he reported, his enhanced vision tracking patterns of power that human eyes could never perceive. "Each mutated site is becoming a focal point, channeling energy into the larger circuit. Like... neurons firing in a vast supernatural brain."

"And the failed transformations?" Sister Angelique asked, her honey-colored eyes grave as she studied her own mystical readings.

"Still rising." Mills forced himself to watch through hybrid senses as more impure bloodlines were culled, their failed metamorphoses feeding a different kind of power into the Comte's machine. "He's using even the failures. The energy released when unstable hybridizations collapse... it's being harvested, refined, fed back into the system."

"Efficient," Marie's ancient voice came through the speaker phone, carrying notes of reluctant admiration. "He's designed it so that every outcome serves his purpose. Success or failure, survival or death – it all feeds the transformation engine."

Marissa moved to study the map they'd been using to track the crisis, her fingers tracing the patterns of power that were now visible even to normal human perception – lines of force connecting each transformation site, forming a vast occult circuit with the Comte's mansion at its center.

"The original murders," she said suddenly. "Elena, Catherine, Marie... they weren't just ritual sacrifices. They were calibration points. Testing the resonance frequencies needed for mass transformation."

"Yes," Mills confirmed, another layer of hybrid insight surfacing. "He needed to fine-tune the harmonics, ensure they would trigger only the bloodlines he'd properly prepared. The brides used their victims to test different combinations, different frequencies of supernatural power..."

His voice trailed off as new hybrid senses detected movement throughout the city – transformed sleeper agents congregating at specific points, their movements guided by instincts written into their blood centuries ago.

"They're gathering," he reported. "The successful hybrids. Forming... concentration points. Places where the power can be focused more efficiently."

Through the phone came the sound of McBride swearing. "Confirmed. Just got reports from the Quarter. They're taking over major intersections, historic buildings, anywhere with mystical significance. And they're... building something. Physical construction overlaid with some kind of energy manipulation."

"The frames of reality itself," Sister Angelique said grimly. "They're creating anchor points where multiple dimensions can intersect. Places where normal space can support the kind of power the Comte's ascension will require."

As if to illustrate her point, Mills' hybrid vision caught glimpses of what the transformed were constructing – devices that seemed to exist in more than three dimensions, their geometries hurting even his enhanced perception to look at directly.

"How many focal points?" Marie demanded.

Mills forced himself to count through the pain of seeing too much reality at once. "Nine major nodes, arranged in a nonagon pattern around the Quarter. Each one staffed by hybrids with specific ability combinations.

Like... specialists, their bloodlines bred to handle particular aspects of the engine."

"And what about the smaller gathering points?" Sister Angelique asked. "The ones forming between the major nodes?"

"Support structures. Places where less stable hybrids can contribute without risking collapse of the main framework." Mills' hands began moving unconsciously, hybrid instincts trying to sketch designs encoded in his blood. "The entire city is becoming a vast energy collection system, designed to—"

He broke off as new awareness flooded his transformed senses. Through the hybrid network spreading across New Orleans, he could feel the Comte beginning the next phase of his plan.

"He's starting the power collection," Mills gasped, fighting against the compulsion to join his fellow hybrids at the nearest focal point. "Drawing energy from every successful transformation, every failed hybridization, every death and rebirth across the city..."

The others felt it too, though their perceptions were limited by human senses. The air grew thick with supernatural power, reality itself straining as forces beyond natural law were channeled through the Comte's carefully constructed system.

"The grimoire," Marie said suddenly. "The one his forces stole from my vault. He's using it to accelerate the process, bypass the need for the eclipse's natural power."

"Because he's discovered something better," Sister Angelique realized. "The energy released by mass transformation, by hundreds of carefully bred bloodlines awakening at once... it's more potent than mere astronomical alignments."

Through his hybrid senses, Mills caught fragments of the Comte's true plan – glimpses of possibilities so vast they threatened his sanity despite his perception.

"He's not just trying to become a god," Mills whispered, ancient knowledge surfacing through generations of encoded memory. "He's trying to rewrite the fundamental laws of reality itself. To create a new framework where hybrid nature is the base state of existence. Where everything is transformed, everything is elevated..."

"How long?" Marissa asked, her warm hand finding his cold one despite the obvious danger of touching a hybrid mid-transformation.

Mills checked his hybrid senses, measuring the power building across the city. "Hours. Maybe less. Once enough energy is collected, once the framework is properly anchored..."

"Then we move now," Sister Angelique declared. "Before his power becomes absolute."

But Mills could feel something else through the hybrid network – awareness of their plans, countermeasures already being implemented. The Comte had planned for this too, had bred specific bloodlines just to handle potential interference...

"We can't," he growled, fighting against hybrid instincts demanding he stop them, prevent them from disrupting the great work. "He's already sent them. The hunter bloodlines. Hybrids specifically designed to eliminate threats to the transformation."

As if summoned by his words, new movement registered on his enhanced senses – shapes flowing through shadows, hybrid powers bent toward a single purpose. The Comte's engineered hunters, coming to ensure nothing interfered with his ascension.

"How many?" Marie demanded.

"Dozens. Maybe hundreds. All from bloodlines bred for combat, for tracking, for elimination of threats." Mills could sense their approach, could feel the resonance of shared blood even through their specialized breeding. "And they're not just coming here. They're moving against everything that might disrupt the progression. Other vampire power centers, witch covens, any organization with the strength to resist..."

"A purge," Sister Angelique said grimly. "Eliminating all opposition before the final phase begins."

"We need to run," Cassie insisted, already gathering her most important grimoires. "Find somewhere to regroup, to plan..."

"There is nowhere," Mills said softly, his hybrid senses showing him the true scope of what was coming. "The hunter bloodlines... they can track through dimensions, follow psychic traces across realities. They won't stop until every potential threat is eliminated."

The implications hung in the air like cemetery mist. They were trapped between hybrid hunters bred specifically for elimination of resistance, and the vast transformation engine gathering power for the Comte's ascension to godhood.

And Mills, carrying one of the Comte's masterwork bloodlines, could feel his own hybrid nature resonating with both sides of the conflict – part of him wanting to join the great work, part of him wanting to help eliminate threats to its completion.

"Mills." Marissa's voice cut through the storm of hybrid instincts. "Stay with us. Fight it."

He tried, focusing on her warmth, her humanity, everything that anchored him against the tide of transformation. But his hybrid senses showed him too much – the patterns of fate drawing them all toward inevitable conclusions, the carefully crafted bloodlines fulfilling their designed purposes...

"We have one chance," he said finally, forcing himself to think past hybrid programming. "The Comte's plan requires perfect resonance between all elements. If we can disrupt even one major node, introduce interference into the energy collection..."

"It would cascade through the entire network," Sister Angelique finished. "Like throwing a wrench into delicate machinery."

"But the hunter bloodlines..." Marie began.

"Will be focused on protecting the nodes, yes." Mills could sense their deployment patterns, their inherited strategies. "But they can't be everywhere at once. And they won't expect one of the masterwork bloodlines to turn against the great work."

The others absorbed the implications of what he was suggesting. Using his hybrid nature – the very tools the Comte had bred into his bloodline – to sabotage the transformation engine from within.

"It's suicide," Sister Angelique said bluntly. "Even with your hybrid powers, going against specially bred hunter bloodlines..."

"We don't have a choice." Mills could feel the power building across the city, reality itself beginning to warp under the pressure of the Comte's machine. "If we don't stop this now, everything changes. Not just New Orleans, not just our reality, but the fundamental nature of existence itself."

Before anyone could respond, his hybrid senses detected new movement – hunter bloodlines, closing in on their location. Their inherited powers were impressive even by hybrid standards, generations of careful breeding culminating in perfect predators.

"They're coming," he growled, fangs extending fully as combat instincts encoded in his own hybrid nature surfaced. "Multiple teams, approaching from all directions."

"How long?" Marie demanded.

"Minutes. Maybe less." He could track their progress through shared blood resonance, feel the deadly purpose in their specialized genetics. "You need to go. All of you. I'll hold them off."

"No." Marissa's voice was firm. "We're not leaving you to face them alone."

"This isn't a discussion." Mills let his vampiric nature show fully now, centuries of carefully bred power manifesting in ways that made reality itself shudder. "I'm the only one who can delay them long enough to matter. The only one whose bloodline might give them pause..."

"Then we go together," she insisted. "All of us. Find a way to disrupt the cellular reformer as a team."

But Mills could see through hybrid senses what was coming – the hunter bloodlines converging on their location, their specialized powers ready to eliminate any threat to the Comte's great work.

The choice was simple, if horrible: stay together and be overwhelmed by superior numbers, or split up and have a chance of disrupting the transformation before it was complete.

"Mills," Sister Angelique said softly, her witch sight obviously showing her something of what was coming. "Whatever you decide, decide quickly. They're almost here."

He looked at Marissa one last time, memorizing her features through his senses that saw too much – the patterns of potential in her blood, the carefully woven threads of fate that had brought them to this moment...

"I'm sorry," he said, and meant it with every cell in his body.

Then he unleashed his blended nature fully, centuries of careful breeding expressing themselves in a burst of power that shattered reality itself.

The last thing he saw before half-bred speed took him away from the sanctuary was Marissa's face – not afraid, but determined. Understanding what he had to do, even if she hated the necessity of it.

The hunt was about to begin.

And somewhere in his mansion on Burgundy Street, surrounded by the fruits of centuries of careful breeding, the Comte raised a final glass of blood in toast to the chaos to come.

The transformation of reality itself was approaching.

And the only one who might be able to stop it was a hybrid who couldn't even trust his own carefully engineered nature.

The real question wasn't whether Mills could disrupt the genetic forge.

The question was: would there be anything left of him to save when it was over?

They were about to find out.

And the fate of not just New Orleans, but existence itself, hung in the balance.

Chapter 15: Blood's Betrayal

The French Quarter bled power.

Mills could taste it in the air – copper and ozone and something older, stranger, like time itself had begun to decay. His hybrid senses registered every facet of the transformation gripping New Orleans: the low thrum of energy being channeled through the Comte's vast machine, the crystalline song of reality straining under supernatural pressure, the whispers of blood calling to blood across generations of careful breeding.

The scents alone threatened to overwhelm his enhanced perception. Incense and grave dirt from impromptu rituals being conducted by successful hybrids. The metallic tang of failed transformations, bodies rejecting blood that didn't match their maker's exacting standards. Beneath it all, the familiar spices and river mud that marked New Orleans, now twisted by forces beyond natural law.

From his position atop St. Louis Cathedral – territory claimed by the brides but temporarily abandoned as they attended their maker – Mills mapped the flow of power through the city. His hybrid vision pierced physical barriers, showing him the true scope of what the Comte had built.

Nine major nodes formed a perfect nonagon, each one a nexus of supernatural energy being channeled by specially bred hybrid bloodlines. Between them, smaller collection points gathered power from successful and failed transformations alike. The pattern was beautiful in its complexity, generations of careful planning expressed in a machine that spanned dimensions.

And at the center, in his mansion on Burgundy Street, the Comte prepared for ascension.

"The eastern node is the weakest," Mills subvocalized, knowing Sister Angelique's spelled communications crystal would carry his words to the others. "The hybrids manning it are newly transformed, their bloodlines less stable than the other points."

"The hunter bloodlines will be concentrating their defense there," Marie's voice came back, distorted by interference from the massive energies being channeled through the city. "They'll expect us to target the obvious vulnerability."

"Which is exactly why we're going to hit the strongest point instead." Mills focused his hybrid senses on the northwestern node, where some of the Comte's oldest and most carefully bred bloodlines maintained a crucial power junction. "They won't expect one of the masterwork bloodlines to attack the elite."

The plan was desperate, probably suicidal. But Mills could feel the change approaching completion through his awareness. Reality itself was beginning to yield under the pressure of the Comte's machine, preparing to accept new laws written in blood and power.

They were out of time for anything else.

"Marissa and Cassie are in position," Sister Angelique reported, her voice carrying traces of strain. Maintaining their spelled communication network through the interference of the transformation engine was clearly taking its toll. "McBride has the police response coordinated – what's left of it. When you move..."

"Everything changes," Mills finished. He could feel it in his hybrid blood – the moment of crisis approaching, when centuries of careful breeding would either fulfill their designed purpose or be turned against their maker's plan.

Movement caught his heightened senses – hunter bloodlines patrolling the rooftops, their specialized genetics expressing themselves in predatory grace. Mills forced himself to remain still, letting hybrid instincts guide him in blending with the shadows despite his new nature.

The hunters passed within feet of his position, their own enhanced senses partially blinded by the massive energies being channeled through the city. Mills caught fragments of their thoughts through blood resonance – inherited memories, encoded strategies, generations of careful breeding focused on a single purpose.

When they were gone, he allowed himself a slow breath that carried a thousand scents: old stone and copper pipes, pigeons and tourist trash, and beneath it all, the heavy metallic tang of power being compressed beyond natural limits.

"Moving now," he subvocalized, letting his speed take him across rooftops toward his target. The northwestern node thrummed with contained energy, reality warping visibly around the focal point where some of the Comte's oldest bloodlines channeled power into his modification array.

His vision showed him the defenses – layers of supernatural barriers maintained by hybrids bred specifically for the task. Guard positions manned by transformed members of security services, their inherited powers bent toward protection of the node. And at the center, the device itself – a construction that existed in more dimensions than human minds could process.

"In position," Marissa's voice came through the spelled crystal, carrying warmth that cut through the cold calculation of his hybrid nature. "Whatever you're going to do..."

"I know." Mills focused his senses on the node, letting hybrid instincts analyze its vulnerabilities despite the part of him that wanted to protect it. "When you see the signal..."

He never finished the sentence. His hybrid awareness screamed a warning seconds before new shapes flowed out of the shadows – hunter bloodlines, their specialized genetics allowing them to track him despite his precautions.

"Well well," their leader said, her voice carrying centuries of careful breeding. "The prodigal son, come to disrupt father's great work." She moved with liquid grace, her own hybrid nature expressing itself in predatory beauty. "Did you really think we wouldn't be watching for you specifically?"

Mills let his hybrid nature surface fully, centuries of encoded power manifesting in ways that made reality shudder. "Alexandra. Still serving as his attack dog after all these years?"

"Better his hound than a traitor to the blood." She smiled, revealing fangs that gleamed with inherited power. "We were there, you know. When he first tasted your bloodline, when he added the final elements to your breeding. Such potential, such careful design... and now you want to throw it all away?"

"He's not creating a new species," Mills growled, hybrid senses tracking the other hunters as they moved to surround him. "He's building a prison. A new framework of reality where everything is bound to his will through blood and transformation."

"Of course he is." Alexandra's laugh was like breaking crystal. "That's the point, little brother. Perfect order through perfect hierarchy. Everyone in their designed place, serving their bred purpose." Her smile widened. "Just like you were meant to serve yours."

She moved faster than even hybrid senses could properly track, her specialized genetics expressing themselves in combat perfection. Mills barely managed to avoid her first strike, centuries of encoded reflexes firing on pure instinct.

The battle that followed was beyond human comprehension. Hunter bloodlines unleashed powers bred into them over generations, their specialized natures turning reality itself into a weapon. Mills countered with his own hybrid abilities, letting inherited combat instincts guide his transformed body.

But he was one masterwork bloodline against six hunter strains, each one bred specifically for elimination of threats to the great work. Even with his superior genetics, the numbers...

Pain lanced through his enhanced nervous system as one of Alexandra's strikes connected, her inherited powers disrupting the carefully crafted balance of his hybrid nature. He stumbled, hybrid speed failing for crucial seconds.

The hunters pressed their advantage, specialized abilities combining to pin him against supernatural barriers he couldn't phase through. Alexandra approached slowly, savoring her victory.

"The Comte warned us you might try something like this," she said, power gathering around her transformed form. "Told us how to handle it if one of the masterwork bloodlines went rogue." Her smile was terrible in its beauty. "Would you like to know what he bred into us specifically for this situation?"

Mills felt it then – resonance between their shared blood, Alexandra's specialized genetics reaching for something buried in his own hybrid nature. Compelling him to...

"No," he snarled, fighting against the inherited programming trying to surface. "I won't..."

"Blood remembers blood, little brother." Alexandra's voice carried frequencies that made his hybrid senses scream in recognition. "And your blood remembers its true purpose."

The pressure built in his transformed nervous system as centuries of careful breeding responded to calls encoded in their shared genetics. Mills felt his blended form turning against itself, generations of designed loyalty warring with conscious choice.

"Still fighting?" Alexandra sounded almost proud. "The Comte chose your bloodline well. Such strength, such determination... it's almost a shame to waste it."

She raised her hand, inherited power gathering for a killing stroke. Mills could sense the perfect harmonics of it – specialized genetics expressing themselves in weapons keyed specifically to disrupting mixed lineage.

Time seemed to slow as merged perception processed everything at once: the hunter bloodlines maintaining their containment field, Alexandra's power reaching for fatal frequencies, the vast energies of the transformation engine humming through reality itself...

And something else. Something even the hunters' specialized senses hadn't detected.

A familiar heartbeat, moving closer despite the obvious danger.

"No," Mills tried to warn, but it was too late.

Marissa stepped out of concealment, her voice carrying power that had nothing to do with genetics: "Get away from him."

Alexandra's laugh was genuinely amused. "The little siren, coming to save her pet hybrid? How... predictably human."

But Mills could sense something the hunters couldn't – power gathering around Marissa that had nothing to do with the Comte's breeding programs. Something older, wilder, rooted in human magic rather than engineered bloodlines.

"Last warning," Marissa said softly. And beneath the words, almost subsonic: music.

The hunters tensed, specialized senses finally registering the threat. But their genetics had been bred to deal with hybrid powers, with carefully engineered abilities passed down through controlled bloodlines.

They had no defense against what came next.

Marissa sang.

The sound bypassed hybrid hearing entirely, resonating directly with the blood that formed the basis of their engineered natures. Mills felt his own genetics responding despite generations of careful breeding – ancient power calling to something deeper than mere biology.

Alexandra screamed as her specialized abilities began to turn inward, inherited powers responding to frequencies that disrupted the very foundations of hybrid nature. The other hunters fell back, their carefully bred defenses useless against magic that preceded the Comte's great work.

"Impossible," Alexandra gasped through fangs that were already beginning to retract. "He bred us specifically to resist... to control..."

"He bred you to resist hybrid powers," Marissa corrected, her voice carrying harmonics that made reality itself vibrate in sympathy. "But I'm not using hybrid anything. This is older. Much older."

Mills felt his own interlinked senses resonating with her song, centuries of careful breeding yielding to something that predated the Comte's experiments. Through enhanced senses overwhelmed by competing frequencies, he watched the hunters' specialized genetics begin to falter.

"The node," he managed through a throat that was trying to transform back to human. "While they're disrupted..."

Marissa nodded once, never breaking the otherworldly harmonics of her song. Mills forced himself upright, fighting through the competing pulls of otherworld awareness and older power.

The node's defenses were already weakening as the hunters lost control of their specialized abilities. Mills gathered every scrap of power he could still access, generations of careful breeding expressing themselves one final time...

And struck at the exact frequency his enhanced senses had identified as crucial to the node's stability.

Reality shattered.

The last thing Mills saw before consciousness failed was Alexandra's face – not angry, but almost relieved as centuries of careful breeding finally yielded to something older than blood.

Then darkness took him, and he dreamed of music that could break the bonds of programmed genetics.

When he woke, everything had changed.

The node was gone, taking a significant portion of the Comte's mutations with it. But the backlash had consequences none of them could have predicted.

The real question wasn't whether they could stop the Comte's ascension anymore.

The question was: what would happen to all his carefully bred bloodlines when the power sustaining their hybrid nature suddenly failed?

They were about to find out.

And somewhere in his mansion on Burgundy Street, surrounded by the fruits of centuries of breeding, the Comte felt his great work begin to unravel.

The real horror was just beginning.

And not even carefully engineered genetics could predict what would happen next.

Chapter 16: Unraveled Destiny

Pain had a color.

Through destabilizing hybrid senses, Mills watched his carefully engineered nature tear itself apart in shades of crimson and void. The destruction of the northwestern node had sent feedback cascading through the Comte's entire network, disrupting the careful balance of power that sustained their transformed genetics.

Every hybrid in New Orleans was feeling it – generations of careful breeding coming undone as the energy that supported their altered nature fluctuated wildly. Mills could sense them through failing blood resonance, hundreds of transformed bloodlines struggling to maintain cohesion as their maker's great work began to unravel.

"Hold him down!" Sister Angelique's voice seemed to come from very far away. "The genetic restructuring is accelerating..."

Mills felt hands trying to restrain his convulsing body – Marissa's warm touch, Cassie's magic-enhanced grip, even McBride's purely human strength. But hybrid nature answered to its own laws, even in dissolution.

"The others," he managed through a throat that couldn't decide if it wanted fangs or normal teeth. "Across the city... they're all..."

"We know." Marie's ancient voice carried real fear. "The destabilization is affecting every transformed bloodline. Some are reverting to human, some are... changing into something else entirely."

His enhanced vision flickered in and out, showing him fragments of the chaos gripping New Orleans: Hybrid powers running wild as carefully engineered genetics tried to compensate for the loss of stabilizing energy. Hunter bloodlines losing control of their specialized abilities, their bred purpose turning inward. And everywhere, the bodies of those whose transformations couldn't survive the sudden shift in supernatural dynamics.

"The Comte," Mills gasped as another wave of genetic restructuring tore through him. "He'll try to... restore the network. Use the remaining nodes to..."

"He can't." Sister Angelique's honey-colored eyes blazed as she worked complex spells meant to slow his dissolution. "The harmonic interference from the destroyed node has contaminated the entire system. Any attempt to channel that much power through the remaining focal points..."

"Would accelerate the destabilization," Cassie finished, consulting her grimoire with shaking hands. "The whole thing's coming apart at a genetic level. The carefully bred bloodlines, the engineered abilities... it's all unraveling."

Mills felt it happening in his own hybrid nature – centuries of selective breeding expressing themselves in increasingly chaotic ways as the power that sustained them fluctuated. One moment he could see through walls and time itself, the next he was barely more than human. His fangs extended and retracted randomly, enhanced senses spiking and failing without pattern.

"There has to be a way to stabilize them," Marissa insisted, her hand never leaving his despite the obvious danger of touching a destabilizing hybrid. "All those people... they didn't ask for this. They didn't choose to be part of his breeding program."

"The siren song," Marie said suddenly. "What you did to the hunters... could it work on a larger scale? Provide an alternative resonance frequency for the transformed bloodlines to lock onto?"

Before Marissa could respond, Mills' senses screamed a warning seconds before reality itself seemed to shudder. Through failing vision, he caught glimpses of what was happening at the Comte's mansion:

The ancient vampire stood in his ritual chamber, surrounded by the most stable of his transformed children. But even they were showing signs of genetic degradation, their carefully bred abilities becoming increasingly unpredictable. The Comte himself seemed to be coming apart at a molecular level, the power he'd gathered for his ascension turning inward as his great work collapsed.

"No," Mills whispered as understanding hit with clarity. "He's not trying to stabilize the network. He's going to..."

The Comte's voice reached through blood resonance, carried on frequencies that made reality itself vibrate in sympathy: "My children. My carefully crafted bloodlines. If we cannot ascend together... we will transform this world through our dissolution."

Power beyond comprehension gathered around the ancient vampire as he prepared to channel the destructive energy of thousands of destabilizing hybrids. Mills could see the truth through failing enhanced senses – the Comte meant to use their genetic unraveling as a weapon, to tear apart the very fabric of reality through the death throes of his great work.

"How long?" Sister Angelique demanded, obviously sensing the buildup of power through her own supernatural awareness.

"Minutes. Maybe less." Mills forced himself to focus through another wave of genetic restructuring. "He's going to use our deaths to fuel something worse than his original transformation. Turn the failure of his great work into a different kind of victory..."

"How many will survive?" Marissa's voice helped anchor him as hybrid nature tried to tear itself apart.

"None of us. Not the hybrids, not the humans... maybe not even reality itself." Mills could feel it building through blood resonance – the Comte gathering the destructive potential of every failing bloodline into a weapon that would remake existence through annihilation.

"There has to be something we can do," McBride insisted. "Some way to..."

He never finished the sentence. New power pulsed through the remains of the Comte's network, causing every hybrid in the city to convulse as their unstable genetics responded. Mills felt his body trying to express every inherited ability at once – telepathy and telekinesis and deeper powers overwhelming his transformed nervous system.

"He's starting," Sister Angelique reported grimly, her witch sight tracking the buildup of destructive energy. "Using the death of his great work to fuel something even larger..."

Mills caught fragments of the Comte's true plan: Reality itself coming apart as thousands of engineered bloodlines destroyed themselves in harmony. The carefully bred traits that were supposed to birth a new species becoming the weapon that would end the old one. And at the center of it all, the Comte preparing to ride the wave of destruction into a different kind of godhood.

"The song," he gasped, looking at Marissa through eyes that couldn't decide if they were human or hybrid. "What you did to the hunters... it didn't just disrupt their abilities. It gave them something else to align with. Something older than hybrid genetics..."

Understanding dawned on her face. "You want me to try it on every transformed bloodline in the city? Mills, I don't even know how I did it the first time..."

"You did it because you had to," he said, forcing the words out through another wave of genetic dissolution. "Because something in you responded to something in us...

something older than careful breeding, deeper than engineered nature..."

"He's right," Sister Angelique said suddenly. "The siren gift... it doesn't just disrupt supernatural harmonics. It can provide new ones. Give the failing bloodlines something to stabilize around..."

"A chance to choose," Mills finished. "To align with something they weren't bred for..."

Another pulse of destructive power tore through the remains of the Comte's network. Mills felt his body trying to tear itself apart in response, centuries of careful breeding expressing themselves in one final catastrophic mutation.

"Decide quickly," Marie advised through their failing spelled communication. "The Comte is almost ready. When he channels the combined death throes of every hybrid in New Orleans..."

Marissa looked at Mills, her eyes showing fear for the first time since this started. "If I do this wrong... if I hit the wrong frequency..."

"Then we die anyway." He managed a smile despite fangs that wouldn't stay extended or retracted. "But we die trying to save something rather than destroy everything."

She nodded once, determination replacing fear. "How do I... where do I..."

"The cathedral tower," Sister Angelique said. "The brides used it to broadcast their hunting song. The acoustics are perfect for supernatural harmonics..."

"No time," Mills growled as another wave of genetic restructuring tore through him. "Has to be here. Has to be now."

Marissa took a deep breath, obviously preparing herself for whatever came next. "If this doesn't work..."

"It will." Mills put every scrap of failing hybrid confidence into the words. "Because it has to."

She nodded again, squeezed his hand once... and began to sing.

The sound bypassed normal hearing entirely, resonating directly with the unstable genetics of every transformed bloodline in New Orleans. Mills felt his hybrid nature responding despite generations of careful breeding – ancient power calling to something deeper than engineered traits.

Through failing enhanced senses, he caught glimpses of the effect rippling across the city: Destabilizing hybrids pausing in their dissolution as new frequencies gave them something to align with. Hunter bloodlines finding purpose beyond their bred nature. Even the Comte's most successful children responding to harmonics that preceded their maker's careful planning.

"It's working," Sister Angelique reported, her witch sight tracking the spread of stabilizing resonance. "The transformed bloodlines are..."

She never finished the sentence. New power pulsed through what remained of the Comte's network – not the frequencies of dissolution this time, but something else. Something worse.

Mills felt it through failing blood resonance: The Comte, realizing what they were attempting, preparing to channel everything he had left into one final working. Not just the death throes of his great work, but the very essence of his own ancient nature.

The real question wasn't whether Marissa's song could stabilize the failing bloodlines anymore.

The question was: could they survive what came next?

They were about to find out.

And somewhere in his mansion on Burgundy Street, surrounded by the ruins of centuries of careful breeding, the Comte prepared to show them exactly why he was considered one of the Original vampires.

Chapter 17: Ancient Blood

The Comte's true power finally revealed itself.

Gone were the carefully crafted plans of genetic manipulation. In their place rose something far older and more terrible – the raw might of an Original vampire, one of the first of their kind. Power that predated science, that laughed at human concepts of biology and breeding.

Mills felt it through the failing connection of shared blood – ancient strength that had nothing to do with engineered traits and everything to do with primal darkness. The Comte was drawing on powers that existed before written history, before civilization itself.

"The blood of ages," Sister Angelique whispered, her witch sight clearly showing her something that made even her ancient knowledge quail. "He's accessing powers that haven't been seen since the first nights..."

Through vision that was rapidly losing its enhanced qualities, Mills watched darkness spread from the Comte's mansion. Not metaphorical darkness, but something deeper

– shadows that ate light itself, that moved with purpose and hunger older than time.

"The first vampires weren't made," Marie's voice came through their failing spelled communication. "They were chosen by powers that predate humanity. The Comte... he's calling on those same forces now."

Marissa's song continued to resonate through the city, offering stability to those caught in the collapse of the Comte's grand design. But even her siren gift seemed to falter as ancient night pressed against reality itself.

"What's happening to them?" McBride demanded, watching through mundane eyes as people throughout the French Quarter fell to their knees, clutching their throats. "The ones who were... changed..."

"They're being offered a choice," Mills managed through fangs that were now permanently extended, driven by powers older than genetics. "Accept the ancient blood... or die as failed experiments."

He could feel it himself – the pull of primordial night calling to something deeper than carefully crafted bloodlines. The Comte was offering everyone he'd touched a chance to embrace an older, purer form of vampire nature.

"How many will survive?" Marissa's voice carried worry even as she maintained the stabilizing harmonics of her song.

"Those who are worthy," Marie answered grimly. "Those whose souls are dark enough to embrace what vampires truly were, before science and breeding programs tried to tame our nature."

Through failing enhanced senses, Mills caught glimpses of the transformation spreading across New Orleans: People who had been part of the Comte's grand design now being remade by forces that cared nothing for careful planning. Some dissolved into ash as ancient power found them wanting. Others... others became something terrible and pure.

"The hunters," he gasped as another wave of primal power tore through him. "Alexandra and her team..."

"Accepting his offer," Sister Angelique confirmed, tracking the spread of ancient night through her witch sight. "Becoming what vampires were meant to be, before the Comte tried to engineer a new species."

Mills felt it happening in his own blood – carefully crafted traits burning away as something older tried to take root. The Comte's voice echoed through powers older than language:

"Join me, my children. Not as engineered hybrids, but as true creatures of the night. Embrace what vampires were before science tried to explain us, before breeding programs tried to perfect us..."

The offer was tempting. Mills could feel the purity of it – power uncomplicated by genetics or careful planning. Simple, primal strength that asked only for complete surrender to eternal darkness.

"Mills." Marissa's voice cut through the ancient call, anchoring him against tides of night that wanted to sweep away his humanity. "Stay with us."

He tried, focusing on her warmth, on the light she represented. But the pull of primordial power was strong, offering release from complexity into pure predatory existence.

"The Comte is gathering them," Sister Angelique reported, her honey-colored eyes tracking movements through supernatural darkness. "Those who accept transformation into true vampires... they're being drawn to his mansion. Forming a court of ancient blood."

Through senses that were becoming more vampiric in the old way, Mills caught glimpses of what was assembling in the Comte's lair: Dozens of newly transformed vampires, their carefully engineered natures burned away and replaced by something older and purer. Alexandra was among them, her specialized breeding replaced by simple predatory perfection.

"He's building an army," Marie said softly. "Not of hybrids or carefully bred bloodlines, but of true vampires. Children of the first night..."

"How many?" McBride demanded.

"Enough." Mills could sense them through shared darkness rather than shared blood now. "Maybe fifty who survived transformation into the ancient form. But each one with power that makes the engineered abilities look like parlor tricks."

As if to prove his point, new strength flooded his supernatural senses – not the carefully crafted powers of hybrid nature, but something deeper. Older. Hungrier. The Comte's voice echoed through primordial night:

"Choose now, my children. Join me in eternal darkness, or perish as failed attempts to improve upon perfection..."

Mills felt his body burning away completely, leaving him balanced between two possibilities: Accept transformation into a true vampire of the ancient blood, or die as a failed experiment in supernatural evolution.

"Mills." Marissa's voice anchored him once more, her song offering a third option – stability through connection to something older than even vampire nature. "Whatever you choose..."

He looked at her through eyes that were struggling between human and ancient vampire, seeing both her physical form and the pure light of her soul. The choice seemed impossible – surrender to primordial night and gain power beyond imagination, or hold onto humanity through connection to her light.

Before he could decide, reality itself seemed to shudder as the Comte gathered his new court for their first hunt. Ancient power pulsed through New Orleans, calling all who had embraced true vampire nature to join in a feast that would remake the city in darkness.

The real question wasn't whether Mills would choose humanity or ancient power anymore.

The question was: could any of them survive what was coming?

They were about to find out.

And somewhere in his mansion on Burgundy Street, surrounded by children of the first night, the Comte prepared to show New Orleans exactly what vampires were before science tried to explain them.

The true horror was just beginning.

And not even Marissa's siren song could fully shield them from powers that predated music itself.

Chapter 18: Night's Children

Darkness had a pulse.

Mills felt it through blood older than history – the rhythmic surge of ancient power as the Comte gathered his newly transformed court. Throughout the French Quarter, shadows moved with predatory purpose as vampires of the old blood answered their maker's call.

"They're hunting in packs," McBride reported through their failing spelled communication. "Taking whole streets at a time. The evacuation..." He broke off, the sound of screaming carrying clearly through the line. "We've lost contact with three emergency response zones."

From Sister Angelique's sanctuary, Mills watched New Orleans succumb to powers that predated civilization. His senses, stripped of engineered enhancements but growing stronger in the old way, showed him the horror unfolding across the city.

Alexandra led one hunting party, her carefully bred nature replaced by pure predatory grace. She moved like living shadow through the panicked crowds, each kill an act of terrible beauty. The others followed her example, embracing their new existence with unholy joy.

"The Comte is channeling their kills," Sister Angelique observed grimly, her witch sight tracking flows of supernatural energy. "Each death feeds his power, strengthens his connection to forces older than time itself."

"How many have turned?" Marissa asked, her hands steady as she worked with Cassie to reinforce the sanctuary's wards. Her other abilities remained firmly in the background where they belonged, irrelevant to the growing crisis.

"At least fifty accepted transformation into true vampires," Marie answered through the spelled crystal. "Each one with power that makes modern vampires look like children playing at darkness. And they're making more..."

Mills caught glimpses through blood-enhanced vision: The newly transformed hunting with terrible efficiency, selecting victims with ancient instinct. Some they killed outright, feeding the Comte's power. Others they chose for the dark gift, adding to their numbers with each passing hour.

"The old ways spread faster," Sister Angelique explained as another wave of screaming marked a successful hunt. "No careful breeding, no engineered bloodlines. Just pure darkness calling to compatible souls."

"And the ones who aren't compatible?" McBride's voice carried horror even through the spelled communication.

"Die in the attempt," Mills said softly, watching another failed transformation through enhanced vision. "The old blood is... particular about who it accepts."

He felt it in himself – the pull between humanity and ancient power growing stronger with each passing moment. The Comte's voice echoed through blood older than language:

"Choose, my son. Embrace what we truly are, or perish as a failed attempt to improve upon perfection..."

"Mills." Marissa's voice anchored him against tides of darkness that wanted to sweep away his humanity. "Stay with us."

He tried, focusing on her warmth, on the light she represented. But the call of ancient night was strong, offering release from complexity into pure predatory existence.

"The Comte is nearly ready," Sister Angelique reported, tracking power flows through her witch sight. "Once he gathers enough energy from his children's kills..."

"He'll try to access the same powers that created the first vampires," Marie finished. "Not to become a god through science and breeding, but through connection to forces that predate human understanding."

Mills caught glimpses of the preparations: The Comte in his mansion, surrounded by children of the night as he gathered power older than history. The ancient vampire's form seemed to shift and flow, becoming something that hurt even supernatural vision to look at directly.

"How do we stop him?" McBride demanded. "There has to be..."

He never finished the sentence. New power pulsed through the city as the Comte began channeling the combined strength of his transformed court. Mills felt it in blood that was becoming more vampiric in the old way – pure darkness unrestrained by modern limitations.

"We can't fight this conventionally," Sister Angelique said grimly as reality itself seemed to shudder under supernatural pressure. "He's accessing powers that existed before human concepts of combat or resistance..."

"Then we fight unconventionally," Marissa insisted. She met Mills' eyes without flinching. "You said the old blood is particular about who it accepts? That it tests worthy souls?"

"Yes," he managed through fangs that were now permanently extended. "The darkness... it has to find something compatible in the victim. Something that resonates with powers older than time..."

"Then we give it something else to resonate with." She turned to Sister Angelique. "The sanctuary's wards – they're based on principles older than vampire nature, aren't they? Protection rituals that predate written history?"

Understanding dawned on the priestess's face. "Yes... the oldest forms of defensive magic, drawing on powers that existed before darkness itself..."

"Can we use them?" Marissa's voice carried determination that cut through supernatural shadows. "Not just to defend, but to fight back?"

Marie's ancient voice came through their spelled communication: "It's possible. Dangerous beyond imagination, but... if we could tap those same primal forces, turn them against powers that prey on humanity..."

Mills felt possibilities shifting through blood-enhanced senses – patterns of power realigning as hope offered an alternative to surrender or destruction. But before they could explore the idea further, new awareness flooded his supernatural perception.

The Comte had felt their resistance. And now he was sending his darkest children to eliminate the threat.

"They're coming," Mills growled, ancient power letting him track movement through shadows themselves. "Alexandra and the strongest of the transformed. The Comte wants us dealt with before we can..."

"How long?" Sister Angelique demanded, already gathering materials for whatever ritual they were planning.

"Minutes. Maybe less." He could feel them through shared darkness now, moving with terrible purpose through a city that was rapidly becoming their natural hunting ground. "And they're stronger than before. The old blood... it grows more powerful with each kill."

The others absorbed the implications, knowing they were almost out of time. The real question wasn't whether they could access powers older than vampire nature anymore.

The question was: could they do it before the children of the night tore them apart?

They were about to find out.

And somewhere in his mansion on Burgundy Street, surrounded by darkness older than history, the Comte prepared to show them exactly why the first vampires were considered gods by primitive humans.

The true horror was just beginning.
And not even powers that predated night itself might be enough to stop what was coming.

Chapter 19: Powers That Predate Night

Sister Angelique's sanctuary thrummed with powers older than darkness itself. Ancient symbols carved into the foundations began to glow with eldritch light as they prepared to tap into forces that existed before the first vampire drew breath.

Mills watched as the priestess and Cassie worked to modify wards that predated written history. His senses, growing stronger in the old way, showed him layers of protection deeper than modern magic could comprehend.

"The original defenses against darkness," Sister Angelique explained as she traced patterns in substances that hurt even supernatural eyes to look at directly. "Not prayers or spells, but pure concepts of protection given form before humans had words for such things."

"Will it be enough?" Marissa helped position ritual elements that seemed to exist in more dimensions than space should allow. "Against powers that created the first vampires?"

"Nothing is enough against such forces," Marie's ancient voice came through their failing spelled communication. "But these defenses... they draw on the same primordial well of power. The light that existed before darkness learned to hunt."

Mills caught glimpses of what they were attempting through senses that grew more vampiric by the moment: Tapping into energies that predated the split between light and shadow, accessing powers that existed when reality itself was young and malleable.

But time was running out. Through blood-enhanced perception, he tracked Alexandra's hunting party as they moved through the French Quarter with terrible purpose. The transformed vampires had embraced their ancient nature completely, becoming something that modern minds couldn't properly comprehend.

"They're splitting up," he reported, watching darkness flow like liquid night through city streets. "Surrounding the sanctuary... they know what we're trying to do."

"The Comte feels it," Sister Angelique confirmed, her witch sight tracking flows of power older than history. "The forces we're accessing... they threaten everything he's built. Everything he hopes to become."

Through their fading spelled connection, McBride's voice carried fresh horror: "The others... the vampires hunting through the city... they're all converging on your location. Leaving their kills, abandoning their territories..."

"Because the Comte commands it," Mills growled, feeling the pull of ancient blood as their maker gathered his children for one final assault. "He wants us destroyed before we can access powers that might actually hurt him."

The implications hung in the air like cemetery mist. They had minutes at most before the full might of the Comte's transformed court descended on their sanctuary. Dozens of vampires empowered by the old blood, led by those who had most fully embraced their ancient nature.

"The ritual isn't ready," Cassie said, desperation clear in her voice as she worked to modify protective circles that had existed for millennia. "We need more time..."

"Time is the one thing we don't have." Sister Angelique's honey-colored eyes tracked movement through walls as darkness pressed against their failing outer wards. "They're here."

Mills felt them through blood older than language – Alexandra and her elite hunters, moving with terrible grace as they tested the sanctuary's defenses. Behind them came others, each kill having made them stronger in the old way. And through it all, the Comte's presence grew as he channeled power through his children's shared darkness.

"The inner chamber," Sister Angelique commanded, already gathering materials they would need. "The oldest wards, the pure concepts of protection..."

They retreated deeper into the sanctuary as reality itself seemed to shudder under supernatural pressure. Mills caught glimpses through enhanced vision of what was gathering outside: Shadows that moved with predatory purpose, darkness given form and hunger by powers that predated civilization.

The first assault on their outer defenses made the entire building shake. Modern wards shattered like glass, centuries of carefully crafted protection spells falling before strength drawn from humanity's oldest nightmares.

"They're stronger than they should be," Marie's voice carried real fear even through the spelled crystal. "The old blood... it grows more powerful with each passing moment. As if something is accelerating their evolution into true creatures of the night..."

"The Comte," Mills realized, ancient knowledge surfacing through shared darkness. "He's not just channeling power through them... he's reshaping them. Making them more perfect expressions of vampire nature with each kill, each act of destruction..."

Another wave of assault tested protections that had stood since New Orleans was founded. Mills felt the shadows probe for weaknesses, seeking any flaw in defenses laid down by those who first fought the darkness.

Alexandra's voice carried through supernatural barriers, beautiful and terrible: "Come out, little brother. Accept what you truly are. What we were all meant to be..."

"Don't listen," Marissa's hand found his in the growing darkness. "Whatever they offer..."

"It's not an offer anymore." Mills could feel it through blood that was becoming more vampiric by the moment – the pull of ancient power, the call of shared darkness. "The Comte... he's done waiting. What comes next..."

He never finished the sentence. New power flooded the night as their maker unleashed forces that existed before human consciousness. Mills felt it tear through his body – pure darkness unrestrained by modern limitations or natural law.

The sanctuary's outer walls began to crack as shadows pressed against stone older than the city itself. Through failing defenses came glimpses of what waited outside: Vampires of the old blood, their forms shifting between human and something far more primal. Leading them was Alexandra, her carefully bred nature burned away and replaced by perfect predatory grace.

"The inner chamber," Sister Angelique insisted as another wave of assault made reality itself groan in protest. "If we can just complete the ritual..."

They retreated to the sanctuary's heart, where the oldest protections still held. Here, symbols carved before written language glowed with power that predated darkness itself. Here, they might access forces that could match what the Comte had unleashed.

But time was running out. Mills could feel the shadows pressing closer, ancient power eating through layers of defense that had stood for centuries. Soon, not even the oldest wards would be enough to hold back the night.

"Choose now, my son." The Comte's voice echoed through blood older than history. "Join us in eternal darkness, or perish as those who cling to failed concepts of protection..."

Mills felt his humanity balanced on a knife's edge as powers beyond comprehension battered at his soul. The choice seemed impossible – surrender to primordial night and gain strength beyond imagination, or hold onto what remained of his mortal nature.

"Mills." Marissa's voice anchored him once more as shadows pressed against the inner chamber's final defenses. "Whatever you decide..."

He looked at her through eyes that were struggling between human and ancient vampire, seeing both her physical form and the pure light of her soul. Mills caught glimpses of possibilities – patterns of fate shifting as choices older than time itself presented themselves.

Before he could respond, reality shuddered as the Comte gathered his full court for one final assault. Ancient power pulsed through New Orleans as every transformed vampire answered their maker's call to destroy those who dared access powers that predated the night.

The real question wasn't whether Mills would choose humanity or ancient darkness anymore.

The question was: could any of them survive what was about to be unleashed?

They were about to find out.

And somewhere in his mansion on Burgundy Street, surrounded by children of the night, the Comte prepared to show them exactly why the first vampires were worshipped as gods by those who huddled in caves, afraid of the dark.

And the fate of not just the city, but of darkness and light themselves, hung in the balance.

Chapter 20: When Darkness Falls

The inner chamber of Sister Angelique's sanctuary blazed with power older than night itself. Ancient symbols pulsed with eldritch light as they accessed forces that existed before the first shadow learned to hunt. Mills watched as reality itself seemed to bend around rituals that predated written history.

Outside, darkness pressed against failing wards as the Comte's children gathered for their final assault. Alexandra led them, her form shifting between human beauty and something far more primordial as the old blood expressed itself fully. Behind her came others transformed by ancient power, each kill having made them stronger in ways that defied modern understanding.

"The seals are breaking," Sister Angelique reported grimly as another wave of supernatural force tested protections laid down by those who first fought the darkness. "Even the oldest wards can't hold them back much longer."

Through blood that was becoming more vampiric by the moment, Mills felt the Comte gathering his power. The ancient vampire was channeling forces that existed before human consciousness, preparing to unleash horrors that primitive peoples had worshipped as gods.

"Join us, brother," Alexandra's voice carried through supernatural barriers, beautiful and terrible. "Accept the gift of perfect night, of power unconstrained by mortal limitations..."

Mills fought against the pull of shared darkness as the Comte's presence grew stronger. He caught glimpses of what was assembling outside: Shadows that moved with predatory purpose, darkness given form and hunger by powers older than civilization itself.

"The ritual," Marissa reminded them as another assault made reality groan in protest. "Whatever we're going to do..."

"Almost ready." Sister Angelique worked with desperate precision, placing elements that seemed to exist in more dimensions than space should allow. "The forces we're accessing... they're delicate. If we rush this..."

She never finished the sentence. New power flooded the night as the Comte unleashed his full strength through his transformed children. Mills felt it tear through his blood – pure darkness unrestrained by natural law or modern comprehension.

The sanctuary's inner walls began to crack as shadows pressed against stone older than the city itself. Through failing defenses came glimpses of what waited outside: Vampires of the old blood, their forms no longer even pretending to be human. They moved like living night, each one a perfect expression of predatory nature.

"Time's up," Mills growled as another wave of assault made ancient wards flare and dim. "Whatever we're going to do..."

Sister Angelique nodded once, determination replacing fear in her honey-colored eyes. "Then we do this now. Ready or not."

She began to speak in languages that predated human speech, accessing concepts of protection that existed when reality was young and malleable. Around them, the oldest symbols blazed with power that made even vampiric vision flinch away.

The Comte felt it. Through blood-enhanced senses, Mills caught his maker's reaction as forces older than darkness itself began to manifest. The ancient vampire gathered his children closer, preparing to meet powers that might actually be able to harm him.

"Choose now, my son," the Comte's voice echoed through shared night. "Stand with your true family as we remake this world in perfect darkness, or perish with those who cling to failed concepts of light..."

Mills felt his body balanced between possibilities as Sister Angelique's ritual reached its climax. Through enhanced vision, he saw patterns of fate shifting as choices older than time itself presented themselves.

The moment of decision arrived as reality shuddered under supernatural pressure. Mills looked at Marissa, seeing both her physical form and the pure light of her soul. The choice seemed impossible – surrender to primordial night and gain power beyond imagination, or hold onto what remained of his humanity.

Before he could decide, the Comte struck.

Ancient power flooded the sanctuary as shadows became solid things, hunting with purpose older than human consciousness. The inner chamber's defenses held for one eternal moment...

Then shattered like glass under forces that predated protection itself.

Darkness poured through the breach as the Comte's children attacked with terrible purpose. Alexandra led them, her form now completely inhuman as the old blood expressed itself without restraint.

The battle that followed defied modern understanding. Sister Angelique wielded powers that existed before shadow, meeting darkness with forces equally primordial. Cassie's magic took on aspects older than written spells, accessing concepts that made reality itself shudder.

And Mills... Mills found himself caught between natures as ancient power surged through his blood. The pull of shared darkness called him to join his maker's children in eternal night. But something else, something older than even vampire nature, offered a different path.

The real question wasn't whether they could survive what the Comte had unleashed anymore.

The question was: what would remain of reality itself when powers this primordial clashed?

They were about to find out.

Chapter 21: Gods and Monsters

The first clash between ancient powers tore reality apart.

Mills felt it - the moment when forces that predated darkness met powers drawn from primordial night. The inner chamber of Sister Angelique's sanctuary became a battleground between concepts that existed before human consciousness could name them.

Alexandra led the Comte's children through the breach, her form now completely inhuman as the old blood expressed itself without restraint. Behind her came others transformed by ancient power, each one a perfect expression of what vampires were before civilization tried to explain them.

"Hold the circle!" Sister Angelique commanded as shadows with predatory purpose pressed against the last remnants of protection. Her honey-colored eyes blazed with power older than light itself as she wielded forces that made reality shudder.

The battle defied modern understanding. Darkness became solid things, hunting with terrible grace as the

Comte channeled strength through his transformed court. But Sister Angelique met them with powers equally primordial - concepts of protection that existed when the universe was young and malleable.

Mills found himself caught between natures as ancient forces surged through his blood. The pull of shared darkness called him to join his maker's children in eternal night. But something else, something that predated even vampire nature, offered a different choice.

"Brother," Alexandra's voice carried frequencies that hurt what remained of his humanity. Her beauty had become something terrible and pure as the old blood reshaped her into a perfect predator. "Accept what you truly are. What we were all meant to be..."

Through blood-enhanced senses, Mills watched the battle unfold on multiple levels of reality. The physical combat was brutal enough - transformed vampires moving with impossible grace as they tested defenses laid down by those who first fought the darkness. But the true conflict occurred on planes that human minds couldn't properly perceive.

Sister Angelique wielded concepts that existed before shadow, her ritual accessing powers that made even vampire vision flinch away. Around her, the oldest symbols blazed with light that seemed to eat darkness itself. But the Comte's children pressed forward, each kill having made them stronger in ways that defied natural law.

"The seals," Cassie warned as another wave of assault made ancient wards flare and dim. "They're failing. The power we're accessing... it's too much for the containment..."

She was right. Mills could see it through enhanced vision - reality itself beginning to tear as forces too primordial for this plane of existence manifested fully. The very fabric of space-time groaned under supernatural pressure.

"Let it fail," Sister Angelique said grimly, her voice carrying harmonics older than human speech. "Let it all come through. If we're going to face gods..."

"Then we become gods ourselves," Marie's ancient voice completed through their failing spelled communication. "Access everything. Hold nothing back."

The priestess nodded once, determination replacing fear as she began to speak in languages that predated civilization. Around them, the oldest symbols pulsed with power that existed when reality was young and malleable.

The Comte felt it. Through blood-enhanced senses, Mills caught his maker's reaction as forces older than darkness itself fully manifested. The ancient vampire gathered his children closer, preparing to meet powers that might actually be able to harm him.

"So be it," the Comte's voice echoed through shared night. "You wish to wage war with concepts that predate consciousness? Then let us show you exactly what the first vampires were before time itself learned to flow properly..."

New power flooded the sanctuary as the Comte unleashed his full strength through his court. Mills felt it tear through his blood - pure darkness unrestrained by natural law or modern comprehension. The ancient vampire's form began to shift, becoming something that hurt even supernatural vision to look at directly.

"Mills." Marissa's voice anchored him as reality buckled under opposing forces. She stood within Sister Angelique's circle of power, her humanity somehow untouched by the clashing energies. "Whatever you choose..."

He looked at her through eyes that were struggling between human and ancient vampire, seeing both her physical form and the pure light of her soul. Through blood-enhanced senses, he caught glimpses of possibilities - patterns of fate shifting as choices older than time itself presented themselves.

The moment of decision arrived as powers beyond comprehension battered at his monstrous nature. The pull of shared darkness called him to embrace what vampires truly were before science tried to explain them. But something else offered a different path - one that required sacrificing power for the chance to remain at least partially human.

Before he could decide, the Comte struck.

Ancient night flooded the sanctuary as shadows became solid things, hunting with purpose older than human consciousness. Sister Angelique's circle held for one eternal moment...

Then shattered like glass under forces that predated protection itself.

What followed defied description in any modern language. The Comte's children attacked with terrible purpose, their forms shifting between states of existence as the old blood expressed itself without restraint. Sister Angelique and Cassie wielded powers that existed before shadow, meeting darkness with forces equally primordial.

And Mills... Mills found himself fighting battles on multiple levels of reality. His physical form moved with vampire grace, meeting Alexandra's attacks as she tried to force his transformation into a true creature of the night. But the real conflict occurred in his blood, where ancient powers waged war for his very nature.

"Choose!" Alexandra's voice carried frequencies that made reality itself shudder. "Choose what you truly are!"

Through failing enhanced vision, Mills caught glimpses of what the Comte was becoming - something that existed before vampires, before darkness itself learned to hunt. The ancient vampire's power reached through blood and bone, trying to remake everything in primal night.

The real question wasn't whether they could survive what had been unleashed anymore.

The question was: what would remain of reality itself when powers this primordial finished their battle?

Chapter 22: Before Night Was Night

The battle between primordial forces tore open the veil between worlds.

Through blood older than history, Mills felt reality fracture as powers that existed before darkness met forces drawn from eternal night. The sanctuary had become a nexus where concepts too ancient for human comprehension waged war for supremacy.

Sister Angelique stood at the heart of their failing circle, wielding magics that predated written language. Her honey-colored eyes blazed with power as she spoke words that existed before humans learned to name the darkness they feared. Around her, the oldest symbols pulsed with light that seemed to devour shadows themselves.

But the Comte's children pressed forward, their forms shifting between states of existence as the old blood expressed itself without restraint. Alexandra led them, her beauty now transformed into something terrible and pure - a perfect predator from humanity's darkest memories.

"You cannot stop what was always meant to be," her voice carried frequencies that made reality shudder. "We are becoming what vampires were before time itself learned proper flow, before light and dark knew their separate natures..."

Through enhanced senses overwhelmed by competing powers, Mills watched the Comte's true form begin to manifest. The ancient vampire had shed all pretense of humanity, becoming something that existed in the spaces between moments. His presence alone made the fabric of space-time groan in protest.

"Behold," the Comte's voice echoed through blood and bone, "what we were before your kind learned to make fire, to push back the eternal dark. When we were gods to those who huddled in caves, afraid of what hunted in endless night..."

New power flooded the sanctuary as the ancient vampire channeled forces through his transformed court. Mills felt it tear through his blood - pure darkness unrestrained by natural law or modern comprehension. Reality itself began to fold under supernatural pressure.

"Hold!" Sister Angelique commanded as shadows with predatory purpose pressed against their last defenses. "The ritual isn't complete. If we can just maintain the circle long enough..."

But the Comte's children attacked with terrible purpose, each one a perfect expression of what vampires were before civilization tried to explain them. Their forms flowed like liquid night, moving through dimensions that human minds couldn't properly process.

Mills found himself fighting battles on multiple levels of existence. His physical form moved with vampire grace, meeting Alexandra's attacks as she tried to force his transformation into a true creature of darkness. But the real conflict occurred in his blood, where ancient powers waged war for his very nature.

"Join us, brother," Alexandra's beauty had become something beyond mortal understanding as the old blood reshaped her into living night. "Accept what you truly are. What we were all meant to be..."

"Mills." Marissa's voice somehow cut through the chaos of competing forces. She stood within what remained of Sister Angelique's circle, her humanity a beacon in the growing darkness. "Whatever you decide..."

He looked at her through eyes that were struggling between human and ancient vampire, seeing both her physical form and the pure light of her soul. The choice that faced him wasn't just about personal survival anymore - it was about what darkness itself would become.

Before he could decide, reality screamed.

The Comte's transformation had reached its apex, accessing powers that existed before the universe learned proper form. Through blood-enhanced senses, Mills watched his maker become something that defied comprehension - a being of pure night from before stars first learned to shine.

"You see now?" The Comte's voice carried frequencies that made existence itself shudder. "This is what we truly are. What we were always meant to be. Before light thought itself equal to darkness, before time knew to flow in just one direction..."

New shadows poured into the sanctuary - not the mere absence of light, but something older and hungrier. The Comte's children moved through these primordial depths with terrible grace, their forms becoming one with powers that predated consciousness itself.

Sister Angelique met them with forces equally ancient - concepts of protection that existed when reality was young and malleable. Around her, the oldest symbols blazed with light that seemed to eat darkness itself. But even these primordial defenses began to fail under the pressure of what the Comte had become.

"Choose now," the ancient vampire's presence filled every shadow, every space between moments. "Choose what darkness itself will become. What night was always meant to be..."

A world remade in eternal night, where darkness ruled unchallenged as it had before the first light dared to shine. The Comte's children hunting through shadows that had forgotten any other state of being. Reality itself reshaped by powers that existed before time knew proper flow...

Or something else. Something that required sacrificing godhood for the chance to remain at least partially human. A choice that might cost him everything, but would preserve the balance between light and dark.

The moment of decision arrived. Mills looked at Marissa one last time, seeing the light in her soul that defied even primordial darkness.

Then he made his choice.

Chapter 23: What Night Remembers

Mills chose humanity.

The decision rippled through realities older than time itself, sending shockwaves through the fabric of existence. Through blood enhanced by ancient power, he felt the moment his choice struck the heart of what the Comte had become – a rejection not just of godhood, but of what darkness itself might be.

The ancient vampire's response shook the foundations of New Orleans.

"Fool," the Comte's voice carried frequencies that made reality bleed. "You would deny your true nature? Reject powers that existed before light dared to shine?" His form shifted between states of existence, becoming something that hurt even supernatural vision to witness. "Then watch as I remake everything in eternal night..."

New shadows flooded the sanctuary – not mere absence of light, but something older and hungrier. The Comte's children moved through these primordial depths with terrible grace, their forms becoming one with powers that predated consciousness itself. Alexandra led them, her beauty now transformed into perfect predatory existence.

"You disappoint us, brother," her voice carried harmonics that made space-time shudder. "We offered you godhood, offered you what vampires were always meant to be..."

"No," Mills stood his ground as reality warped around them. "You offered slavery. Surrender to powers that would remake everything in eternal darkness."

Sister Angelique seized the moment, channeling forces equally ancient through symbols that existed before written language. Around her, the oldest forms of protection blazed with light that seemed to devour shadows themselves.

"The choice is made," her honey-colored eyes blazed with power older than history. "The balance must be maintained. What was sundered must be rejoined..."

The Comte's laughter shook the foundations of existence. "Balance? There was no balance before your kind learned to make fire. Only eternal night, only perfect darkness..." His presence filled every shadow, every space between moments. "I will remind reality itself of what it once was..."

The sanctuary's walls began to dissolve as primordial night ate through stone and spell alike. Even Sister Angelique's oldest wards started to fail under pressure from what darkness had been before time knew to flow in one direction.

But Mills felt something else stirring – not the pull of shared darkness or the call of ancient power, but something deeper. Something that remembered what night had been before it learned to hunt, before light and shadow knew their separate natures.

"You speak of what was," he faced his maker as reality trembled around them. "But you've forgotten what night truly was before the divide. Before darkness learned to fear the light..."

Understanding dawned in Sister Angelique's ancient eyes. "Yes... before the separation, before the eternal war between shadow and flame..." Her voice carried harmonics that made existence itself resonate. "When all was one, when night and light were the same thing..."

The Comte's children faltered as power older than their maker's memories stirred. Alexandra's perfect predatory form flickered as something beyond even primordial darkness touched her transformed nature.

"Impossible," the Comte's presence contracted slightly, his godlike power meeting forces it had forgotten could exist. "That time is gone, that unity destroyed when light first dared to shine..."

"No." Mills let the oldest memories flow through blood that was becoming something neither human nor vampire. "It's still there, in every shadow that remembers being light, in every flame that recalls its darker nature..."

Around him, reality began to shift as powers older than the divide between light and dark manifested. The sanctuary's failing wards suddenly blazed with new purpose as symbols that predated written language accessed forces from before the separation.

"The choice was never between light and darkness," Sister Angelique's voice carried understanding older than time itself. "It was between division and unity, between eternal war and remembered wholeness..."

The Comte's children felt it first. One by one, perfect predatory forms began to shift as something beyond primordial night touched what they had become.

Alexandra's beauty transformed again, but not into the terrible grace of a perfect hunter. Instead, her form flickered between states that existed before light and dark knew to be enemies. "What... what is this? This power..."

"What night remembers," Mills answered as forces older than the divide flowed through his blood. "What darkness was before it learned to hate the light..."

The Comte's godlike presence contracted further as powers he had forgotten could exist manifested in his carefully crafted domain. "No... I forbid this. Reality itself will be remade in eternal night..."

But it was too late. Through blood enhanced by memories older than time, Mills felt the change spreading across New Orleans. The Comte's children, transformed by ancient power into perfect predators, were remembering what they had been before the separation. Before night learned to hunt and light learned to burn.

Sister Angelique's voice carried harmonics that made existence itself sing: "Let what was sundered be rejoined. Let what was divided remember wholeness..."

Reality shuddered as powers older than the divide between light and dark fully manifested. The sanctuary's walls became transparent as forces from before the separation rewove the fabric of existence itself.

The Comte's final scream shook the foundations of time and space as memories older than his godlike power touched what he had become. His presence, drawn from darkness that existed before stars learned to shine, met forces that remembered when night and light were one.

The ancient vampire's form began to unravel as unity older than division touched powers he had thought supreme. Through blood enhanced by memories beyond time, Mills watched his maker's godhood dissolve in the face of what darkness truly had been.

"Remember," his voice carried frequencies that existence itself recognized. "Remember what we were before the divide, before eternal war between shadow and flame..."

The transformation spread through every being touched by the Comte's power. His children, remade as perfect predators, found their natures shifting as memories older than night itself awakened. Alexandra's beauty became something that existed before the separation, neither light nor dark but both and neither.

Reality itself began to heal as forces from before the divide rewove what eternal war had sundered. The sanctuary's walls solidified as symbols that predated written language accessed powers older than time.

And somewhere in his mansion on Burgundy Street, surrounded by shadows that remembered being light, the Comte faced the ultimate truth:

That darkness itself remembered what it had been before division.

That night recalled when it had been one with light.
That powers older than time itself remembered unity.
The true transformation was just beginning.

And not even gods could stop what came when existence remembered wholeness.

Chapter 24: When Light and Dark Were One

The Comte's scream echoed through dimensions older than time itself as memories of unity touched what he had become. His godlike form, drawn from darkness that existed before stars learned to shine, began to dissolve as powers he had forgotten could exist manifested in his carefully crafted domain.

Mills watched reality reshape itself around forces that remembered when night and light were one. The sanctuary's walls became fluid as symbols that predated written language accessed powers from before the great divide.

"This cannot be," the Comte's voice carried frequencies that made existence shudder. "I am darkness incarnate, night as it was before light dared to shine..." But even as he spoke, his presence contracted as memories older than eternal night touched what he had claimed as absolute power.

Alexandra and the other transformed vampires felt it first – their perfect predatory natures responding to forces that recalled unity before division. One by one, their forms began to shift as something beyond both light and darkness awakened in blood older than history.

"What's happening to us?" Alexandra's beauty fluctuated between states of being that existed before the separation. "This power... it's not just light or dark..." Her voice carried wonder mixed with fear as memories older than vampire nature stirred in her transformed blood.

"Remember," Mills spoke with harmonics that reality itself recognized. "Remember what we were before night learned to hunt and light learned to burn. Before eternal war divided what was meant to be whole..."

Sister Angelique's honey-colored eyes blazed with understanding as she channeled powers that predated the sundering. Around her, the oldest symbols pulsed with energy that was neither light nor shadow, but something that remembered when such distinctions had no meaning.

"Let what was divided recall unity," her voice carried frequencies that made existence sing. "Let what was sundered remember wholeness..."

The transformation spread through every being touched by the Comte's power. His children, remade as perfect expressions of eternal night, found their natures shifting as memories older than darkness itself awakened. The very shadows that filled the sanctuary began to change, recalling what they had been before division forced them to choose between light and dark.

But the Comte fought against remembering. His presence, drawn from powers that existed before stars first shone, lashed out with forces that threatened to tear reality apart rather than recall unity.

"I am the night eternal," his voice shook the foundations of existence. "I am darkness as it was meant to be, before light presumed equality..." Raw power poured from his unraveling form, trying to remake everything in pure shadow.

Mills stepped forward. "No. You are what night became after the divide. After shadow forgot it had once been one with light..."

The Comte's assault struck him with forces that should have annihilated both body and soul. But Mills felt something beyond physical form respond – not hybrid nature or vampire power, but understanding that existed before such distinctions had meaning.

"Impossible," the ancient vampire's presence contracted further as powers he had forgotten could exist manifested through his chosen heir. "I remade you in eternal darkness. Shaped you to be perfect night..."

"You shaped me to be what you thought night should be," Mills corrected. "But something in me remembered. Something that recalled when light and dark were one..."

Sister Angelique seized the moment, channeling energies that predated written language through symbols that remembered unity. Around them, reality began to heal as powers from before the separation rewove what eternal war had sundered.

The Comte's children felt their natures shifting. Alexandra's perfect predatory form became something that existed before the divide – neither light nor dark but both and neither.

"Brother," her voice carried wonder as understanding touched what she had become. "This is... this is what we were always meant to be. Before eternal night, before the sundering..."

Mills nodded as forces older than time itself flowed through blood that remembered unity. "Before war between shadow and flame. Before light and dark forgot they were one..."

The Comte's scream shook dimensions as powers he had thought supreme met forces that recalled what existence had been before division. His godlike form, drawn from darkness that existed before stars learned to shine, began to unravel as memories older than night itself touched what he had become.

"Remember," Mills spoke with harmonics that reality itself recognized. "Remember what night truly was before it learned to fear the light. Before shadow forgot it could shine..."

The transformation spread through every being touched by the Comte's power. His carefully crafted domain began to shift as forces from before the divide reshaped what eternal night had claimed. The very fabric of existence seemed to heal as memories older than time itself awakened.

Reality shuddered as powers beyond comprehension manifested in the sanctuary. Sister Angelique's voice carried frequencies that made existence itself resonate: "Let what was sundered be rejoined. Let what was divided remember wholeness..."

The Comte's final assault struck with forces that threatened to tear New Orleans apart rather than allow remembering. But something older than his godlike power responded – not through violence or dominion, but through memories of when light and dark were one.

Mills felt the moment unity touched what his maker had become. The Comte's presence, drawn from darkness that existed before stars learned to shine, met powers that remembered when night had no need to hunt.

The ancient vampire's scream echoed through dimensions as memories older than eternal night reshaped what he had claimed as absolute truth. His godlike form began to dissolve as forces from before the divide rewove reality itself.

"Remember," Mills spoke one final time as powers older than time flowed through blood that recalled unity. "Remember what we were always meant to be..."

That darkness itself recalled what it had been before division.

That night remembered when it had been one with light.

That powers older than time itself could not be denied their unity.

The true transformation was almost complete.

Chapter 25: What Power Remembers

The final transformation shook New Orleans to its foundations.

Through blood that remembered unity, Mills watched as time itself reshaped reality around them. The Comte's carefully crafted domain began to dissolve as forces from before the divide between light and dark manifested fully.

The ancient vampire's presence, drawn from eternal night, fought against remembering what darkness had been before division. His form twisted between states of existence as memories older than stars touched what he had become.

"I deny this," his voice carried frequencies that made dimensions bleed. "I am night eternal, darkness supreme..." But even as he spoke, his power contracted as understanding older than shadow itself flowed through what he had claimed as absolute dominion.

Around them, the sanctuary's walls became transparent as symbols that predated written language accessed forces that remembered wholeness. Sister

Angelique stood at the heart of their circle, channeling energies that existed before light and dark knew to be enemies.

"The rejoining cannot be stopped," her eyes blazed with power older than history. "What was sundered remembers unity. What was divided recalls wholeness..."

The Comte's children felt it first – their perfect predatory natures responding to memories that preceded vampire existence. Alexandra's beauty transformed into something that existed before the separation, neither light nor shadow but both and neither.

"This is what we truly were," her voice carried wonder as understanding touched what she had become. "Before eternal night, before the great divide..." Her form flickered between states of being that remembered when such distinctions had no meaning.

Mills stepped forward as forces older than time flowed through blood that recalled unity. "Remember," he spoke with harmonics that reality itself recognized. "Remember what we were before war between shadow and flame. Before light learned to burn and dark learned to hunt..."

The Comte's final assault struck with power that threatened to tear existence apart rather than allow remembering. But something beyond physical form responded – not hybrid nature or vampire strength, but understanding that existed before such divisions had meaning.

"You cannot deny what power itself recalls," Mills faced his maker as reality trembled around them. "What darkness remembers. What night knows in its deepest nature..."

He felt the moment unity touched what the Comte had become. The ancient vampire's presence, drawn from shadows that existed before stars learned to shine, met forces that remembered when night had no need to hunt.

Reality itself began to heal as powers from before the divide rewove what eternal war had sundered. The sanctuary's walls solidified as symbols that predated written language accessed energies older than time.

The transformation spread through every being touched by the Comte's power. His children, remade as perfect expressions of eternal night, found their natures shifting as memories older than darkness itself awakened. The very shadows that filled the sanctuary began to change, recalling what they had been before division forced them to choose between light and dark.

Sister Angelique's voice carried harmonics that made existence sing: "Let what was sundered be rejoined. Let what was divided remember wholeness..."

The Comte's final scream echoed through dimensions as memories older than his godlike power touched what he had claimed as absolute truth. His form, built from darkness that existed before stars first shone, began to dissolve as forces from before the divide reshaped reality itself.

"Remember," Mills spoke one last time, "Remember what we were always meant to be..."

That darkness itself recalled what it had been before division. That night remembered when it had been one with light. That powers older than time itself could not be denied their unity.

The transformation was complete.

Mills felt it the moment when existence itself recalled what it had been before the divide. Around them, reality settled into new patterns as forces from before the separation rewove what eternal war had sundered.

Alexandra and the other vampires found their natures shifting into something that existed before such distinctions had meaning. Neither creatures of pure night nor beings of light, but something that remembered when such divisions were meaningless.

"What happens now?" Marissa's voice grounded Mills as powers flowed through his blood. "What do we become?"

"What we were always meant to be," he answered as understanding touched what the Comte's power had awakened. "Before eternal night, before the great divide... when light and dark were one."

Sister Angelique's eyes held ancient wisdom as she surveyed what their ritual had wrought. "The balance is restored. Not through eternal war between shadow and flame, but through remembered unity..."

The sun rose over New Orleans, painting the sky in colors that existed before light and dark knew to be enemies. And in its light, those who had been touched by the Comte's power found themselves transformed not into creatures of pure night or beings of perfect day, but into something that remembered when such distinctions had no meaning.

The war between light and darkness was over.

Not through victory or defeat, but through remembrance of what power itself had always known:

That unity preceded division. That wholeness came before separation. That light and dark were one before time itself learned to flow.

And in the heart of the French Quarter, where ancient power still lingered in the spaces between moments, reality itself remembered what it had been always meant to be.

~The End~

Patti Petrone Miller

About Patti

Ladies and gentlemen, step right up to "Where the Magic Happens" - a literary circus that'll make your bookshelf do backflips!

Meet Patti, the ringmaster of this wordy wonderland! She's not just an Executive Producer; she's a word-wrangling wizard, conjuring up an animated TV series based on "ELLIOT FINDS A HOME." It's the tail-wagging tale of a thumbs-up pup and his silent sidekick, proving that you don't need words when you've got opposable digits and a heart of gold!

Hold onto your bestseller lists, folks! This Polygon Entertainment superstar has hit the USA TODAY jackpot and Amazon's #1 spot more times than a cat has lives. With 7 dozen books under her belt, she's got more genres than a chameleon has colors. From Urban Fantasy to Horror, she's been spinning yarns longer than your grandma's knitting needles!

But wait, there's more! Patti's life is like a celebrity bingo card:

She rocked "Romper Room" at 4, probably making the other kids look like amateur rompers.

She rubbed elbows with Captain Kangaroo and Mr. Green Jeans. (No word on whether the jeans were actually green.)

She shared a train ride and a sandwich with Sidney Poitier. Talk about a meal ticket to stardom!

Patti Petrone Miller

She high-fived President Nixon at the circus. Who knew the circus could get any more political?

She went to school with David Copperfield. We assume she didn't disappear during attendance.

She roller-skated with pre-famous John Travolta. Grease lightning, indeed!

She sipped cocoa with Abe Vigoda. Fish never tasted so sweet!

When she's not busy being a literary legend, Patti's juggling roles faster than a circus performer. Teacher, grandma, furparent - she does it all with a smile that could light up a haunted house.

knitting needles!

But wait, there's more! Patti's life is like a celebrity bingo card:

She rocked "Romper Room" at 4, probably making the other kids look like amateur rompers.

She rubbed elbows with Captain Kangaroo and Mr. Green Jeans. (No word on whether the jeans were actually green.)

She shared a train ride and a sandwich with Sidney Poitier. Talk about a meal ticket to stardom!

She high-fived President Nixon at the circus. Who knew the circus could get any more political?

She went to school with David Copperfield. We assume she didn't disappear during attendance.

She roller-skated with pre-famous John Travolta. Grease lightning, indeed!

She sipped cocoa with Abe Vigoda. Fish never tasted so sweet!

When she's not busy being a literary legend, Patti's juggling roles faster than a circus performer. Teacher, grandma, furparent - she does it all with a smile that could light up a haunted house.

Speaking of haunted houses, meet the "Queen of Halloween" herself! This Wiccan High Priestess is stirring up stories spookier than a skeleton's dance moves. Her books are flying off the shelves faster than witches on broomsticks, so follow her on social media or risk missing out on the hocus-pocus!

So, come one, come all, to Patti's phantasmagorical world of words! It's more exciting than a roller coaster, more magical than a rabbit in a hat, and more diverse than a box of assorted chocolates. Don't be shy - step into the spotlight and join the literary party where the pages turn themselves and the stories never end!

www.ingramcontent.com/pod-product-compliance
Lightning Source LLC
LaVergne TN
LVHW041810060526
838201LV00046B/1196